Mr Philip Henderson

The Betrayer

Michael Hennessey

2 * The Betrayer

The
Betrayer

Michael Hennessey

The Acorn Press
Charlotetown
2003

The Betrayer
© 2003 by Michael Hennessey
ISBN 1-894838-03-3

This is a work of fiction. Although based on an actual case, the principal characters depicted here are purely imaginary and any similarity to real people is purely coincidental. The facts generally follow those revealed during the trial, but, for story purposes, the author has taken liberties with these as well. Some real names and real institutions and firms are mentioned, but they are peripheral to the main story and are used only for purposes of authenticity.

Cover image: *Colourful Character*, oil on canvas, by Brian Burke
Editing: Jane Ledwell
Design: MCKY
Printing: Transcontinental Prince Edward Island

The Acorn Press gratefully acknowledges the support of The Canada Council for the Arts' Emerging Publisher Program; and the Prince Edward Island Department of Community and Cultural Affairs' Cultural Development Program.

National Library of Canada Cataloguing in Publication

Hennessey, Michael
    The betrayer / Michael Hennessey.

ISBN 1-894838-03-3

        I. Title.

PS8565.E5843B48 2003   C813'.54   C2003-902905-0
PR9199.3.H4525B48 2003

The Acorn Press
PO Box 22024
Charlottetown, Prince Edward Island
Canada C1A 9J2

To the memory of three old friends:

Thomas Edward "Ted" Flanagan,
who always claimed he knew the true identity
of the third man;

Ivan "Fat" Connors,
whose memory for names, dates, and places would
shame a professional historian; and

Ivan "Nailer" Murnaghan,
who prodded me for years to write something about
this case.

✻ ✻ ✻

* PART I

CHAPTER 1

The girders of the new Canadian National Hotel offered temptations few could resist. For weeks the steelworkers of the Halifax contracting firm of R. S. Allen Ltd. had been working overtime, the pneumatic hammers of the riveters pounding from early morning until well into twilight. Now the framework rose above us, the last light of the summer day seeping through the empty spaces against the sky, magnifying this gigantic six-storey structure.

✳

I had crammed sneakered toes and fingers into whatever crevices I could find and was shinnying up tentatively behind Frankie Hanlan. He was older and more confident, and by folding himself into a vee was able to walk up the structure, a feat I couldn't master. We were at the fourth-floor level when I began to tire.

I paused to look around, hooking my arm over a ten-inch girder, my gaze sweeping out towards the harbour. The view was said to be magnificent from up here, but it was already too dark to see anything other than the weak streetlights flickering through tree branches. The glare of large lamps situated strategically brightened the construction site, their aim being to prevent not only theft of materials but also just such idiotic escapades as the one we were embarked on.

"Don't look down, Mickey!" Frankie called sharply from above as he saw me pause. Just then the watchman, old Digger Higgins, looked up. He had been on the far side when we started our climb, but had now worked his slow way around to a spot below us.

"Who's up there?" he shouted. "Get the hell down out of that!"

I glanced down, and that was my undoing. In the fore-shortened view I had of him, old Digger seemed tiny, the wheelbarrow beside him a toy for a child. I suddenly felt my head swimming, and at the same instant my toes`slipped from their hold, leaving me dangling by my right arm.

"Oh Jesus!" I wailed. "I'm slipping!"

"Hang on!" I heard Frankie above me and instinct took over. I grabbed my right hand with my left and hung there, feeling numbness already beginning in my right arm, my stomach cramping with fear as those groping feet that seemed to belong to someone else found nothing but empty space.

✳

I have no memory of time, of what was said. Dimly I recall hearing shouting below, but little else. Then, in what must have been only seconds, I felt Frankie's hand on my shoulder, steadying me, then on my belt as he slid below me, yanking me along the girder, and I could feel the taut skin on my bare arm pinch and tear as I froze in my terror, his quiet, confident tones saving me from complete panic until we finally came to a corner.

"I'm here," he said from below me. "I'm going down ahead of you. Don't look down."

I thought I'd never be able to unlock my fingers, but once I reached the corner and had my legs wrapped around that vertical girder, and once the soothing cadences of Frankie's voice had stilled my terror, I began to respond, saying that I was all right now, that everything was okay, just give me a minute.

"Follow me down," he said. "Put your foot on my shoulder." And we began the agonizing descent, at first only an inch or two at a time as I refused to take either hand or foot off the girders, but, as I became surer, moving in little sliding lurches down the structure.

Old Digger had at last ceased shouting and watched us, positioning himself where we'd land, four feet of broomhandle in his fists. We stopped at the first floor and Frankie climbed up beside me.

"He's waiting to kick the shit out of us," he whispered in my ear. "Here's what we'll do."

As we came down the last few feet, the old watchman cocked the broomhandle like a baseball bat. "I'm going to teach you young bastards a lesson. Come on!" He hit the girder a couple of whacks with the stick, warming up, bracing himself.

He was an old fart of a man with glassy eyes and a rubbery face that could easily go one way or the other depending on what he thought you wanted. There was little joy in his life, and it could have meant his job if an accident occurred. Jobs were scarce, and I suppose he was worried about all that; still, neither Frankie nor I had any desire to get clobbered with a broomhandle.

"Sorry, Dig," Frankie said, and dropped and swung himself off the girder in one fluid movement, landing feet-first into Dig's chest, knocking him spinning and wheezing on his backside into a pile of gravel. I jumped the remaining few feet and darted around the gravel, reaching out to give old Dig a slight knock alongside the head as I passed, and then we were running along Pownal Street past St. Joseph's Convent, chuckling, the sweet smell of summer in my nostrils, the joy of being alive almost more than I could bear.

Behind us we heard the old man shouting, "...and don't come back!" and I began to laugh, clutching at Frankie's arm, laughing uncontrollably until it turned without me knowing it into crying, and Frankie put his arm around me awkwardly and patted my back until I was able finally to begin chuckling again through my gulps and hiccups. "Old Dig'll never forgive you," I said.

"He'll be in tomorrow for a drink," Frankie said — his father was a bootlegger — "and he'll laugh about it. Your arm okay?"

He pointed to where a small trickle of blood was pooling at the crook of my elbow. At that moment amputation would have seemed minor surgery. "It's nothing," I said, wiping it away, the tough street punk again, but realizing at the same moment that in all the excitement I'd wet my pants. When I got home, I said nothing to my mother, but went straight to the bathroom and rinsed out my pants and underpants myself.

✳

I have lived in fear for much of my life, but I was never again to be so terrified as I was that time swinging four storeys above the crepuscular streets of Charlottetown.

Nothing more was ever said of that incident by either Frankie Hanlan or myself, but from that moment on I felt a sense of proprietorship — almost ownership — about that hotel. I had had a life-and-death experience there, and forever after I felt I had more right to it than any of its owners: the CNR, or later Carl Burke, or later still, David Rodd.

I was there at the official opening of the hotel in all my raggedy-assed wonder, drifting around the fringes of the crowd.

In the run-up to the opening there was a big parade from the foot of Queen Street, with the top trotters and pacers of the day leading off: Billy Cope, Lucky Lindy, Longset, Alworthy. But what really attracted me and many others — we all knew about horses — were the cars that followed. For a town the size of Charlottetown, it was amazing the variety of cars that came chuffing up the hill on Queen Street to level off at Hughes's corner, then down to the Fire Station, left on Kent Street past the Police Station, the hotel, Rochford Square, West Kent School, the Drill Shed, Government Pond to the park.

Even today I see those cars on that bright sunny mid-April day as I stood in the doorway of Toombs Music Store: their polished, gleaming bodies glistening against the fading banks of slush and snow piled along the sides of the street, the drivers laughing and waving, honking their horns, enjoying themselves, creating murmurs of wonder and enjoyment, of envy and jealousy. And the cars: the Graham-Page, Chrysler, Plymouth, Durant, Dodge, Willys Knight and Willys Six (Rankin MacLaine, agent), Nash, Hudson, Essex, Hupmobile, Packard, DeSoto, Ford, Chevrolet, Pontiac, Buick, Cadillac, LaSalle, their thin tires mashing down the horse manure, spreading the seeds, laying out a feast for the street sparrows and pigeons. And I watched the birds feed, admiring the machines, knowing that there would never be enough money in my life or the lives of the tattered crowd lining the streets to own one, our bellies gnawing as the feasting sparrows reminded us of how little we'd had to eat that day.

On the night of the hotel opening, the gathered crowd watched silently and respectfully as the officials entered. When they were all inside, the crowd shuffled, uncertain. There was nothing else to do. Then the smart remarks and snickering started.

"Did y'see the get-up on the Governor? Going to a Hallowe'en party."

"What about that daughter of his? Got her mask on already."

"Christ, the women. Those dresses would keep my family in groceries for a year."

"The Mayor better get me that job on the City. My money helped pay for that feast he's eating."

"Poor Billy'd go goddam hungry if he was depending on your money to feed him."

Gradually they faded away. But I hung around, climbing

up to peek in the dining room window, seeing the movement but unable to hear anything but the rattle of dishes, the murmur of voices, the soft tinkle of a piano which I read about the next day in the copy of *The Guardian* I stole from Jimmy Powers's newsstand. The piano, the paper said, was a Heintzman, world-famous, and favoured by the Toronto Conservatory, which possessed ninety-nine uprights and thirty-three grands of that make.

I studied all the details about the opening, even to reading a poem boxed on the front page and written by Mrs. Frances E. Purdie of Winnipeg, no doubt a wife of one of the CNR officials — or at least so I surmised after reading the poem, the first stanza of which remains imprinted on my mind in the corner reserved for such oddities.

> *Island! that in beauty resteth*
> *On the waves of Eastern sea,*
> *Abegweit — (so named by Micmac) —*
> *Art so very dear to me.*

Mrs. Purdie probably lived to regret ever putting pen to paper. But maybe not, since versifying was a favourite pastime of the day, and I imagine the applause that greeted her reading at the official opening would have convinced her that she was a worthy successor to Burns and Masefield, and that her efforts, full of condescension, were appreciated by Islanders.

I gazed skyward at what we called the salt-and-pepper shakers at the corners of the hotel, trying to picture myself inside as one of the privileged, then shook my head at my own fevered imagination.

✳

Writing about Frankie and the hotel makes memory irrevocable. But this is not the story of me and Frankie Hanlan, although he later figured dramatically and drastically in my life. Nor is this the story of a hotel, although it was a place where, periodically, events important to me occurred. This is really my story — Mickey Casey who became Mickey Corcoran who became Hugh Michael Casey.

I have no high motives in writing my story. There is little I wish to claim credit for, nor have I a desire for immortality. Truth to tell, now that I'm retired from my job as a newspaperman, I find the act of writing — what I've done all my adult life — about the only thing that gives me a sense of accomplishment, that allows me some peace of mind, that, perhaps, fulfills the desire we all have to leave something behind, some proof that our lives were something other than wasted.

Why not stick to the positive and ennobling aspects? I have seen the obit they'll run in the paper — I was asked to correct it — and it contains the usual Rotarian details about contributions to the community, good deeds, charity.

Balls. All balls. Well, not all, I suppose. In fact, mostly true. But nothing of the dark side, even if that played only a small part in my life. Are shame and regret really necessary? When I work it out, my wayward activities, if I may call them that, would occupy how long? Six months of a lifetime? No, closer to three. Three months. Can a man be condemned for indiscretions that occurred over three months when he has lived, let's say, a total of 60 years, 720 months? For maybe three months out of a span of 720, I strayed. A mere fraction of my life — one two-hundred-and-fortieth — 1 over 240. A small — Christ, an infinitesimal — bit of my life.

When one is constructing a fiction around oneself one naturally wishes it to reflect as favourably as possible. But if that, then, is the fiction, the lie, do I owe it to anyone to somewhere record the truth? If I do not, is my whole life then a fiction and does God have any part in it?

I have always believed in intervention in our lives — divine or diabolical. Our split personalities don't come about by accident. We are not all good or all evil, but capable of extremes in either direction with an ease that defines us as something other than the creatures of God we are taught we are. If there is no Divine guidance, then it is just as easy to rape, to kill, as it is to be kind and considerate. Easier, since without God there is then no guilt, no fear of retribution, no self-doubt, no obsequiousness.

It is not easy in a small town. In a small town everybody knows you or knows about you. The community celebrates births, marriages, deaths with a quick run through the family tree so that there is a feeling that we are all contained in a huge paper bag which is shaken every now and then, and upended, and one of us falls out. In the meantime, all of us inside the bag live communally with no secrets, acting out the destiny ordained by the community, ending up, unless we struggle, as a small headstone in one of the local cemeteries, with some benighted clergyman standing over us labouring to paint our pathetic lives as something other than what they were.

And if we struggle, if we rebel, we have two choices: leave, or develop a hidden life. Most choose the latter. Oh, we conform, we accept the fatalism that permeates our small, tight world, we become marked for life, but underneath that, or alongside that, or inside that, there develops the quirk, the rebel spirit, the grotesque, kept under control most of the time but forced into the light every now and then, amorality glistening off him, the barometer of his emotional nature, as someone said, "set for a spell of riot."

For years I have seen men and women whose lives were ruined by respectability, domesticity, marriage: people who have lived under such tension in the prison of social conformity that they ended up going to pieces, doing desperate things, destroying themselves and those around them. These are people who embrace suppression and who end up in our mental wards because, when they come to realize the futility of their lives, they snap.

The argument here, of course, is that instead of smothering our sinful natures as Christianity teaches, we'd be healthier if we vaulted out of our hamster cages of respectability and exercised our free will in the enjoyment of what we are taught is sinful.

Well. Who knows? Who cares?

Three lousy months!

CHAPTER 2

By the time I was fifteen I had earned my spurs on the street and commanded respect, which came about as the result of three things.

First was the time I spent at my first paying job, where I learned the value of hard work.

Second was the education I received at Queen Square School, where I learned to hit first and fight quick and mean and dirty.

And third was in the death of the man who claimed to be my relative, where I learned the joy — the sheer uplifting of spirit — of revenge.

But before anything else, what made my experiences possible was growing up in the orphanage.

I had a mother but no recollection at all of my father if, indeed, he was ever around. In the early years I lived with my mother, Elizabeth Casey, in a couple of rooms on Dorchester Street in the West End down near the Charlottetown Hospital. We had a window box for a cooler and a hot plate for a stove. But it wasn't a matter of having things — you don't miss what you don't have. My mother was a warm, sweet person — gentle, with an overall innocent air that people took advantage of. At least that's my read on it from the distance of years.

She had a job of sorts in Doyle's Confectionery. The owner, Aloysius Doyle, was some sort of relative, and Mother worked for him until she had a severe breakdown and had to quit. She didn't talk to me about it, but, unknown to her, when she and her closest friend, Mary O'Malley, were head-to-head one day over coffee and cigarettes, I was hiding behind the couch, even then a little sneak and eavesdropper.

I was too young to understand such expressions as "all over me" and "hands like an octopus," although I have a feeling now that I did have some inkling of what was going on, or at least I understood enough to know that it wasn't good. I certainly knew it was not a paean of praise for Aloysius Doyle I was hearing, and, when Mary insisted, "You have to get away from that," I had visions of my mother deserting me.

When the time came for her to go, she took me to the nuns at St. Vincent's Orphanage, and there I spent the next few years getting a proper education.

They say it's very hard for a child to get used to the loss of a parent, and that's correct up to a point. I know I'll never forget the day my mother dropped me off, her tearful goodbye, the look in her eyes as she watched me from the back seat of the taxi as it pulled out the lane from the Orphanage. I'll see her often, I thought, yet her goodbye seemed so final.

"Be a good boy," she said. "Work hard, listen to the nuns, get your schooling. Always remember that I love you."

She broke down then and held me close. I know I should have cried and begged her not to go, or to go but to keep me with her, but a part of me was standing aside, observing this scene, admiring my stoicism, my bravery, and when I did not cry I saw out of the corner of my eye the two nuns who were there to receive me glance at each other and shrug slightly with a brief fluttering of their shoulders. I felt then and there that I was being singled out as different. Not exceptional different, just oddly different, as if some vital part of me were missing, as if the emotions I should have felt were somehow lacking, and this realization came to me not as a feeling of inferiority — not as if I was missing anything at all — but as a power I had that others had not, a lack of softness perhaps, something that gave me extra strength.

I never saw my mother again.

I went to the orphanage school, and, under the tutelage

of the nuns, like the child Jesus Himself, I "grew and waxed strong."

St. Vincent's Orphanage was a red-brick four-storey building constructed in 1914 across the road from St. Dunstan's University, and run for ten years by the Grey Nuns from Quebec, so-called because of the drab grey habit they wore. They were the poorest of the poor, often reduced to begging from door to door in Charlottetown, a true case of the luckless begging from the hapless, the have-nothings from the have-less. They had been brought to Charlottetown by Bishop Peter McIntyre to look after the Catholic hospital when it was founded in 1879, and subsequently they tended the orphanage. But by 1924 they were forced to withdraw their services from the province. By this time, Bishop Louis O'Leary was in charge, stern and white-haired with the appearance of health, but a man with a delicate, dyspeptic constitution. He turned to the recently founded Sisters of St. Martha, mainly young Island women, informing them that it wasn't a question of whether or not they'd take over the orphanage and the hospital, it was a question of how soon.

With the calm confidence for which they became noted, the Marthas decided that God — or fate in the person of the Bishop — had chosen them for this social service, and they embraced it in the way the Marthas faced every challenge: enthusiastically, unselfishly, with untiring and dedicated devotion, realizing, without the Bishop's caustic reminder, that obedience was one of their vows and that this meant obedience not only to their Superior but also to their diocesan boss, the O'Leary himself.

All institutions have distinguishing characteristics, and just as there is a smell that distinguishes jails and another that distinguishes hospitals, so too orphanages had their own distinct odour. It was not the sour smell of poverty — the nuns had too much spit-and-polish for that. It was something that caught at the back of the throat, that gave off an air, not of hopelessness, for there was always a bright air of optimism about the place, but of something that floated in the atmosphere: a sense of doubt, perhaps, a sense of impermanence. It may have emanated from the mass aura of the children themselves, their sense of loss, their sense of guilt, their sense that somehow, for some reason they couldn't understand, they were not good enough for ordinary family relationships. Whatever it was, anyone who has ever visited an orphanage will tell you that it was there, distinct, palpable, as noticeable as off-meat at a barbecue.

But it did nothing to hold back the work of the Marthas. Much has been written in recent years about what went on in orphanages, but what went on in St. Vincent's was a lot of love, a lot of caring, a lot of education. Oh sure, we got a clout on the ear every now and then, but that was the way things were done at the time. "Spare the rod and spoil the child" was an oft-repeated maxim in the society of the day, and, if some parents used this as an excuse for brutality in their homes, it was something we didn't have to face at St. Vincent's.

I liked to imagine that I had nothing to do with my mother dumping me in the Orphanage, but, while guilt has not been something I have often been troubled with, there is this niggling doubt — a constant from the day Ed's Taxi departed down that lane at six o'clock on a late fall evening, leaves falling, already darkening, the bite of winter in the air, my mother's face in the window fading up the lane, my stomach turning over, my face showing nothing — that somehow I was the cause of it all, of my mother going away and leaving me....

I was generally quiet in this new environment, but my quietness, which originally sprang from shyness, gradually developed as I learned how silence could be used to pursue my own ends while ostensibly agreeing with whoever at the moment was proposing something else. Some people later called me sly and devious and unpredictable, and said such things as, "Don't let the baby face fool you," but I knew that by turning my wide-eyed innocent gaze on my accusers and smiling, I could disarm them and continue to fool at least some of the people some of the time.

✳

It was at the orphanage I first met Emily Kate Ryan, a fiery redhead from the country — Vernon River or Summerville or somewhere like that.

Emily Kate, ah, Emily Kate, who was to be my sister, my confidante, my first love. How can I explain about Emily Kate Ryan without sounding like some pious jerk? I have no wish to paint myself blacker than I was, but the fact was that even as some part of me liked her — admired her, was kind to her — another part of me was calculating how I could use her to my advantage.

It was Emily Kate who took me in hand, showed me the ropes, kept the others from taking advantage of me. I wondered how she exerted such influence until one day I found out — when Billy Williams was trying to shove me around.

It wasn't complicated, simply a case of you-show-me-yours-and-I'll-show-you-mine, and I learned at a very early age that in those games girls always hold the upper hand. Most boys from childhood have little compunction about waving the sign of their masculinity around in front of each other or anyone else; with girls it's the opposite: they create desire by hiding it, by making it mysterious, by giving it an almost holy air. When as young adults we compare notes, we say we learned about sex not from our parents or teachers or any adults, but from our teenage peers. The truth is we were learning about it from our earliest contact with the opposite sex. From treating girls as "one of the boys," to hating them, to taunting and teasing them, to the wonder of what we felt in our loins when near them, to desire and fulfillment, the fact is that in childhood the hunt begins, the chase is on, the drive takes over. It is as natural as our other bodily functions, and, if we are lucky, it remains with us until death, flagging somewhat as we reach what are termed the golden years, but a constant, though by then perhaps more honoured in the breach than the observance.

And when Emily Kate turned Billy Williams from a bully about to pummel me into a grinning idiot simply by swirling her skirt and showing her drawers, I took it in, registered it, and filed it for future reference.

My love of verse, of poetry, also came from Emily Kate who'd been reared in a home where at least Kipling, Thomas Moore, and Longfellow were known. I never knew if the people were her real parents or not, but they had read to her, or, perhaps, being a precocious child, she had read herself to the point where she had committed great chunks to memory.

In the heat of the summer we would play down in the orchard behind the orphanage when occasionally she would suddenly stop whatever she was doing and wander away by herself, and when I approached her warily she would murmur:

> *Life is a waste of wearisome hours*
> *That seldom the rose of enjoyment adorns,*
> *And the heart that is soonest awake to the flowers*
> *Is always the first to be touched by the thorns.*

The first time I heard this, I looked at her with a new respect. "Wow!" I said. "That's great, Emily Kate!" an expression I often aimed at her, both to hide my awe of her and to poke fun at her. "What's it mean?"

She looked down at me from the height of her two-year advantage. "You're too young to understand," she said, her face all serious. "When you get older...."

I said nothing more at this point, but over the next couple of years, as she continued to imply that the world would eventually open to me, I began to develop my own defence mechanisms. I'd give her my hooded look, eyes half-closed, smiling with my mouth only, the aim being to look menacing, threatening.

The first few times she laughed outright at my posturing, but then one day said:

And when you labour to impress, I will not doubt or scoff,
Since I myself have done no less — and sometimes pulled it off.

From that point on she began to help me with suggestions: to keep my own counsel, to avoid the obsequious smile, to keep physically still when confronted, not to become agitated, to nod as if I understood even if I didn't, to have nothing whatever to do with adults if at all possible.

Oh, I was an apt pupil, and Emily Kate with the red hair, the flashing eyes, the freckles, the turned-up nose, the generous mouth, the slightly bowed legs in the beige ribbed stockings, Emily Kate was the teacher every youngster dreams of.

One day I said to her, "I'm going to get out of here."

She looked at me calmly. "Do you have a plan?"

"I'm working on it." I hadn't even thought about a plan. "I'll try to get a job outside."

I saw the doubt in her eyes. "Not as easy as you think."

"I know. It'll take time."

"Don't tell anyone else."

"Why not?"

She stared at me and raised and lowered her eyebrows. "Do I have to tell you?"

I snorted. "No. I guess not." I quoted back at her, "'There's always someone just looking for a chance to take advantage.'"

She smiled fondly at me. "I know it sounds cynical, Mickey, but it's the only way to get along in a place like this where everything you say or do is watched and commented on by others."

She put her arm around me and squeezed. I liked the way it made me feel.

"You're a grand pupil, Mickey," she said. "Just grand."

Clear of the love for my Mother — which at that point in my life was beginning to fade into an aching sore — my love for Emily Kate was the purest I was ever to experience. I adored her. I would literally have died for her.

One night, Emily Kate, Billy Williams, and myself were in the kitchen just off the refectory, where we weren't supposed to be, cadging some extra cookies and milk. If we were caught, we'd catch hell and a lecture, and, worse, we'd be confined to our dorms in our off-time for the next week. Stealing food, even cookies, wasn't a minor offence when almost every bite was measured. There was no extra food and little waste in the orphanage.

I saw a slight movement, a breaking of a moonbeam, through the slide used to pass the food from the kitchen into the refectory. It was raised about two inches, letting reflections in. I "shhhed" the others, and we hunkered down and crept up to the slide, wondering if we'd been caught. What we saw frightened us.

The money for the milk was left each week on a table near the door to the kitchen so that the milkman would get it on his early-morning trip through to the big icebox in the kitchen. What we saw was one of the men who did odd jobs around the place, Tommy Nugent, pick up the money, take a sneaky look around, shove it in his pants pocket, and take off.

We looked at each other. "The dirty crook," Emily Kate said. "We'd better tell Mother Superior before he gets away."

"Wait a minute," Billy said. "We tell her, he'll deny it,

he'll say we were down here and took the money ourselves, and are just trying to blame him."

I nodded. "Billy's right. First thing she'll do is ask what we were doing here at this time of night."

Emily Kate raised her nose to look down at us as only she could. "So we get punished for stealing some milk and cookies. That's no big deal. Stealing money is. There must have been about twenty dollars there. That's a lot of money — more than a man earns in a week."

"Look," Billy said, "I'm not a squealer."

"Neither am I," I said.

"Well, neither am I," said Emily Kate angrily. "But this is not squealing. He stole the orphanage money."

"I see that," I said. "How about this — we get him tomorrow when he comes to work and make him pay it back."

"Sounds good to me," Billy said. "We're big enough to give him some trouble if he refuses."

I knew the promise of possible violence would appeal to Billy, but Emily Kate had reservations. "He'll just laugh at us," she said. "Then where will we be?"

The next day we caught up with Tommy Nugent out front, just before noon. Nugent was a small, wiry man who wore bib overalls and did handyman jobs around the orphanage. He could turn his hand to carpentry or plumbing or electrical problems, and was an asset since something always needed fixing.

"We saw you, Tommy," Billy said.

His tight, weasel face stared at Billy. "Saw me where?"

"In the refectory," Billy said. "Last night."

"We saw you take the money," I said.

"What money?"

"The milk money."

"You're crazy."

"No," I said. "We saw you, and we want you to put it

back."

"If you do, we won't say anything," Emily Kate said.

He laughed. "No little twerps can talk to me like that," he said, and reached over and slapped my face.

Billy was on him in a moment, and I was right behind. We piled on top of him, and we were rolling around on the ground when Mother Superior bustled along.

"What's going on here?" she demanded. "Stop that!" Her voice was like iron. We untangled and stood up.

"Now," she said, "what's this all about?"

"They're blaming me for something they done themselves," Nugent said.

Emily Kate spoke up. "That's not true, Mother. We saw him last night stealing the milk money in the refectory. We were in the kitchen and saw him through the slide."

"I did not!" Nugent shouted. "I wasn't even there!"

"Last night?" The Superior said. "What were you three doing in the kitchen?"

Emily Kate looked away. Billy said, "We know we shouldn't have been there. We were after some cookies and milk. But we didn't take no money. He did."

"Liar!" Nugent shouted. "It's all lies, Mother. I don't know why they'd do this to me."

"*Did* you take the money?" she asked him.

"No! I swear. They must have taken it themselves."

"Did you?" she asked, turning to us.

"No, Mother," Emily Kate said.

"No, Mother," I said.

"No, Mother," Billy said. "He did."

Mother Superior held her job because she was able to make decisions. She made one now.

"Here's what we're going to do," she said. "Nothing. There's no proof either way. So I want you all to go your own way, and I don't want to hear about this matter again. You three into my office now. We'll talk about stealing food."

Nugent looked at us and smirked. We slunk away, not absolved, somehow or other feeling guilty about it all.

The Superior warned us about stealing food, giving us the lecture about taking it from someone else's mouth if we were too greedy. What was a surprise to us was that she didn't restrict us to our dorms in our free time. All she said was, "Now, get out of here, and keep out of the kitchen."

But somehow or other, the word spread. Don't ask me how news spreads in a place like the orphanage. The bush telegraph is always active, and facts are embellished. No one in the dorm can cough without the word being in the refectory a half-hour later that he or she's down with the flu.

In no time, the word was out that we'd stolen the milk money, and we were punished by the only method our peers had for punishment — we were ignored, we were shut out, no one spoke to us. The term "in Coventry" was unknown to us, but that's what we endured. No one would even answer us or listen to our side of the story. We had only ourselves, and each day we hung together in our misery, telling each other that we'd be vindicated in the end.

When the Superior heard about it, she spoke at the evening meal one day, telling the others that what they were doing was wrong, that we had not been blamed for stealing the money. It made no difference. The others were smart enough to know the difference between, "they've not been blamed," and "they're innocent." In their minds, we were still tainted, and some of them, I'm sure, were happy to see the usual paragon, Emily Kate, get blamed for something whether she was guilty or not.

We spent a miserable two weeks, but we grew closer, and I even came to regard Billy with less spiteful eyes. He became more human, bearing up under this cloud, keeping cheerful for Emily Kate's sake.

"We can't let her get discouraged," he said to me. "We have to keep her spirits up."

I was getting pretty down myself. "Yeah?" I said. "Why?"

Billy looked at me in surprise. "What's wrong with you? You know we're innocent. You can take this stuff, and so can I. It's harder for Emily Kate."

I regretted my cynical and pessimistic outburst. I always suspected Billy of having ulterior motives. I found it hard to accept his compassion.

"You've changed," I said, eyes narrowed.

"Just trying to take this as good as I can," he said. "I'm not trying to be goody-goody. I know it'll go away sooner or later. I just don't want Emily Kate hurt."

"Neither do I."

"Well then?"

"Okay," I said grudgingly. "We'll keep her spirits up."

"And each other," he said, patting me on the back. It was the first time a touch from Billy Williams hadn't caused a bruise.

I wasn't enthusiastic about trying to cheer Billy up, but he was never down that I could see. Billy was the kind of guy who seemed to thrive on adversity, who seemed at his best when others were in league against him, as if he were constantly working in an "I'll-show-you" way, remaining cheerful, as if knowing this would baffle his enemies.

It ended as abruptly as it began. Two weeks later, the Superior spoke to the whole orphanage one morning at breakfast, telling us that the night before she had caught a man stealing the milk money. She had waited in the kitchen with the slide up, and she had witnessed the man come in and pocket the money. She confronted him, and when she threatened him with the police, he'd capitulated and turned over the money. As well, she got a confession from him for the first theft and a promise to pay it back in return for her promise not to go to the police. The man, she said, would not be working here any longer. She didn't name him, but everybody knew it was Tommy Nugent.

The Superior concluded her remarks this way: "For the past two weeks, three of our members have been wrongfully subjected to a cruel form of punishment. They are completely innocent, and I am telling you that this treatment will cease *as of now!*"

She sat down and there was a moment of silence. Billy and Emily Kate and myself, who had taken to sitting by ourselves at a table near the door, were gradually engulfed in a wave of well-wishers making half-grudging, embarrassed remarks like, "We knew you didn't do it."

We could have been excused if we'd ignored them, said, in effect, to hell with you all, but we were so relieved, so happy that this exile was over, that we were all near tears, grateful that we were being accepted once again.

It is true, being held to the fire can sometimes bring out the best in a person. Billy bore up under our ordeal better than Emily Kate or myself. Maybe it was because we had never been tested before — we had always gotten along with the others, whereas Billy was often an outsider, disliked for his attitude. I don't know, maybe knowing that Billy had more inner resources was enough to make me resent him then and later on in life. But our joint hardship had bound us together, in a way that would keep us somehow tied to each other, even later on when hatred moved into the picture.

✳

Isolation wasn't the only thing that brought Emily Kate and Billy Williams and myself together. We had another experience that cemented us to each other. It came after one of Emily Kate's "adoptions." She had been taken from the orphanage twice before, but had been returned both times.

Once was because she refused to knuckle under to the woman of the house, and be, in effect, her slave; the other, which we weren't supposed to know about, was when some sexual advances were made to her by the adult male, a matter the good sisters took care of in their own way.

This last time, Emily Kate went to a family in Charlottetown, a Mr. and Mrs. Ned Furlong, who had a fifteen-year-old son. Emily Kate was to be "a sister for little Teddy."

It turned out that "little Teddy" was an overweight bruiser who, within a week, attacked Emily Kate, beat her badly, and tried to rape her, being interrupted and stopped by his father. The Furlongs waited a couple of weeks for Emily Kate's bruises to pretty well heal, then brought her back, reporting to the Superior that she seemed unable to get along with their Teddy.

The Superior was anything but stupid, but while she may have suspected something irregular, she could prove nothing. The parents saw to it that the Superior had no opportunity to speak to young Teddy alone, and every attempt at trying to pry something out of Emily Kate was met with silence, or such expressions as, "We just didn't get along," or, a bit of the truth, "I hated that bully of a son of theirs."

This made the Superior almost certain that something had gone wrong, but without some evidence, or some specific charges, her hands were tied.

Ours weren't. Emily Kate was not so reticent with us, but, while not forthcoming, she answered our questions and admitted that Teddy Furlong had attacked her. When Teddy's father stepped in, he turned his anger on Emily Kate, calling her "a young whore" who had seduced his son. Seeing his way out, Teddy fed this same story to his mother, and they all stuck to it. The last couple of weeks she was there, waiting for her wounds to heal, Emily Kate said they hardly spoke to her except to order her around, and Teddy just sneered and smirked at her the whole time.

I have never seen Billy so mad as when Emily Kate told us this. He smashed his fist into his other hand and swore revenge. "We'll get that bastard," he said. "We'll make him pay."

Emily Kate had by now almost come to terms with her treatment. "He's older and bigger than you, Billy," she said. "Anyway, I don't want you getting into trouble because of me."

Billy looked at me. "We can both take him, Mickey and me." He patted my shoulder. "What d'you say, Mickey? Are you game?"

"Sure," I said, feeling safe since I was convinced Emily Kate would never allow us to do what Billy proposed. "Sure. I'm with you, Billy."

"You'll do no such thing," Emily Kate said. "And that's the last I want to hear about it."

It was the last she heard about it, but it wasn't over for Billy. He kept after me until finally I agreed, and, one night, right after supper, we stuffed our beds with blankets to make them look like someone was in them, and we sneaked away.

We were in luck. We lay in wait on Douglas Street in a gangway across the street from the Furlongs' house. We could see the parents and Teddy through the windows where they had not yet pulled down the blinds.

"He's big," I said.

"He's fat," Billy said. "We can take him easy."

Within an hour, we saw Teddy in the front hall pulling on a jacket and a salt-and-pepper cap and leave. We followed him down by the old Holy Redeemer Church on Upper Queen Street. He turned south to Stewart Street then west past the old Rectory Hall where we rushed him, tumbling him over the four-foot fence around the church property and onto the lawn. We jumped over the fence on top of him.

Teddy Furlong wasn't all fat. He hit me with a right hand over my left eye, and I knew I'd have at least one shiner in the morning. But I got a lovely right uppercut into his breadbasket that almost lifted him off his feet. Billy took a solid blow to the nose that spurted blood over us all, and Furlong fell back for an instant.

"You broke my nose, you bastard," Billy snarled, and walloped the bigger boy with a right he hauled up from his socks. By the time it was over, we were all pretty well marked up, scratched and scraped, but it was Teddy Furlong who was on the ground. As we walked away from him, Billy gave him a half-hearted kick in the gut and said, "That's for Emily Kate."

Back at the orphanage, we cleaned up as best we could and crept into bed. There was no way we could hide the signs of battle, so the next morning, with the connivance of the other boys in the dorm, we staged a mock battle before we went down to breakfast. When we appeared in all our busted-up glory we were marched before the Superior without even being allowed to eat.

"All right," she said. "What happened?"

"We had a disagreement," I said.

"I can see that," she said drily.

"But it's all over now," Billy said.

"I see," she said, looking from Billy to me and back again. "And just what was the disagreement about?"

"It was nothing, Mother," I said. "It's over."

"It was stupid," Billy said. "We were hardly even awake. But we've made up." He held out his hand. "Isn't that right, Mickey?"

"Right, Billy," I said, taking his hand. "No hard feelings at all."

We were making this up as we went along. The Superior looked at us suspiciously. "It doesn't feel right," she said.

"You're holding back something. Does this have anything to do with Emily Kate?"

"Hardly, Mother," Billy lied.

"Why would it, Mother?" I said.

The Superior knew the difference between an outright denial and an evasion, but she let it slide.

"Don't let it happen again," she said. "I mean it. Now get out of here." She turned to some paperwork on her desk.

Outside, we smiled at each other, fellow conspirators. "It was a good plan," Billy said.

"Maybe. Wait'll Emily Kate sees us."

She took one look and started laughing. "You," she said, pointing at me. "You look like a raccoon with those shiners." Both eyes had coloured up, the left one worse than the right. "And you," she said pointing at Billy's swollen and reddened nose. "If you could play that horn, you'd outdo Harry James."

But by the time the three of us wandered off alone, she grew more serious. "Okay," she said. "You can tell me what happened."

We'd already agreed, Billy and I, that we'd not tell her about our trip into town.

"It was nothing," I said. "You know how those things build up. One fella says one thing, the other another, and all of a sudden they're into it."

"I couldn't even tell you what started it," Billy said. "One minute we were just hollering at each other, the next we were at it."

Like the Superior, she regarded us suspiciously, but said only, "Okay, then, it's over?"

"It's over," I said.

"And there's no hard feelings," Billy added.

"Your dorm mates seem to think it was pretty funny," she said.

"I guess it was," Billy said.

If there was a mystery, or if anyone else wondered, the answer came that afternoon when the Furlongs dragged their son into the Superior's office. Like me, Teddy had two black eyes, as well as a bandaged nose, and cuts and scrapes on his face and knuckles. He was bent over, as if nursing a broken rib.

They spent a half-hour in the Superior's office, voices raised at first. But by the time they left, they seemed pacified. It wasn't long before Billy and I were back in front of her again.

"I'm not going to ask you any more questions," she said. "If you had anything to do with beating up Teddy Furlong, I want you to remain absolutely silent. I want no denials, no lies, no deceit. If you're guilty, say absolutely nothing. I do not want our girls going into houses where they might be brutalized, or worse, any more than you do. I have honestly told the Furlongs that not one of our boys has admitted anything nor acted suspiciously. Whoever beat Teddy — two boys, he said — told him it was for Emily Kate. I know neither of you would be so stupid as to say that, so, that's all. Now get out of here before my conscience gets the better of me."

We left, almost tripping over ourselves in our haste, having said not one word, but leaving it clear that we were as guilty as sin.

The grapevine was working overtime and within an hour the whole place knew of the Superior's talk to us, the news probably carried by young Rat Mason who was sneaking away as we left her office. Anyway, we were seen as heroes, as two who had stood up against the outside. Teddy Furlong was the symbol of all we had never had in our lives — power, home, contentment — and we had struck a blow for the deep-rooted resentment orphans feel for those from supposedly "normal" homes. We all felt pretty good about it.

Except, it seemed, Emily Kate. She pulled us aside and said, "I don't need you two idiots beating up on people to help me."

We protested. Billy said, "Nobody is going to do what he did while we're around."

"All you know what to do is fight," she said. "There're other ways."

"Yeah," I said. "Talk."

"Subtlety is beyond you," she snapped. "Don't do it again."

We slunk away, our good intentions in tatters around us. It was some time before we heard the story of how the Sisters, without speaking a word against the family, had quietly by innuendo demolished the man's credibility and reputation, forcing them to move. It was an awesome display of power.

CHAPTER 3

We had work to do at the orphanage, and my early-morning task was to meet the milkman and store the many bottles of milk in the huge icebox. The milkman was Joe Gallant, a happy-go-lucky Acadian, slight of build, a cigarette always drooping from the corner of his mouth, an adult who felt no need to lord it over me or anyone. We were soon on a first-name basis, and it was Joe who told me of the after-school opening at his plant, of how his boss had told him to be on the lookout for a likely boy to take on the job of "corker" as he called it — topping up the bottles and putting in the cardboard stoppers.

"Ain't nothing to it, Mickey," he said. "They pay you fifty cents for three hours' work after school and the same on Saturday. Six days a week — three dollars. What d'you say?"

Money of my own and a chance to get out — naturally, I jumped at it! But first it had to be cleared with Mother Superior, who appreciated industry and ambition and the acceptance of responsibility, and besides, Joe told me, the owner of the milk plant was a cousin of hers, so the feeling that I'd be in good hands was a natural one.

And so I became — by the process well understood by people with names like Baker, Taylor, Butler — Mickey the Corker, Mickey the Cork, Mickey Corker. I became Mickey Corcoran one day after a year on the job when I was in town early and came careening out of the Five and Ten and straight into the arms of Police Sergeant Dominick Murphy.

"What's your name, boy?"

"Mickey Corker-ummm."

"Corcoran?"

I nodded.

"You one of Tom Corcoran's?"

I barely moved my head but it was enough. The Irish sense of persecution was not dead in the Charlottetown of those days, and a sense of unity still prevailed.

"Well, let me tell you one thing, Mickey Corcoran," he said, giving me a quick frisk, feeling the hardness of the Sweet Marie bar in my sleeve but passing it over, "if I ever see you inside this store again, I'll tell your father — and all he'll do is murder you."

My thought was that Tom Corcoran was a hard man, but I had no time to reflect on this.

"Now get out of here," the Sergeant roared and gave me a swift boot in the backside to help me on my way.

It was a lesson I never forgot. Not the kick in the pants — although that was to remain a sore point with me for three days — but the demonstration of how power worked. Magnanimity did not come easily to me — I had little opportunity to exercise it — but I knew I'd remember Sergeant Murphy with gratitude, and I noted in my mental filing cabinet how kindness and compassion could be weapons in my arsenal, to be trotted out and used whenever I felt the need of an ally.

✳

The job was a success for me, and I had some money of my own. I often wandered around uptown either before or after work, and one day I entered Doyle's Confectionery where my mother had worked, noting immediately that all the candy was in glass cases, making it inaccessible to quick fingers. My unformed idea was to try to find out something about my mother without giving myself away. When the bell over the door sounded, Aloysius Doyle shuffled out of his back room, a three-day beard on his wrinkled face, his eyes bleary, the boozy smell of him wafting over the counter.

"What?" he barked.

"Sweet Marie."

"Five cents."

I laid the nickel on the top of the glass; he picked it up and laid down the bar. His blank eyes swept my face.

"Don't I know you?"

"I don't think so."

"What's your name, boy?"

"Mickey Corcoran."

He leaned over to study me, and I backed away from his breath. The eyes sharpened.

"Corcoran, my arse. You're Liz's boy."

"Do you know where my mother is?" I asked politely.

His huge fist slammed down on top of the glass; it quivered, and the candy inside jumped. I marvelled at how he knew just how hard he could hit it without breaking it. An angry man, I thought. One day it will break, and he'll curse its quality.

"Left me up shit creek without a paddle," he muttered. "The bitch."

I gave him my silent, threatening look. If he was impressed, he hid it well.

"Took off to the other side," he said. "Halifax...someplace. No one knows where."

I said nothing and after a few seconds turned to go.

"Wait a minute," he called. "Mickey, is it?"

I nodded.

"How'd you like a job, Mickey?"

"I got a job."

"Doing what?"

I explained it to him.

"I mean a real job. Here. You could stay here, go to school, work after school and on Saturday."

"How much?"

"Two dollars a week."

"I already get three."

"But I'd be feeding you and keeping you. And you'd be out of that orphanage — and living with a relative."

How many divergent paths do we face in our lifetime? How do we decide which way to go? Is it because we have some great master plan before us that indicates that we should take this route, avoid that? I could never subscribe to that theory of a planned life, although I have known people who from their childhood knew the way they'd go and followed that path rigorously. For myself, it has always seemed a matter of the moment. I had no great plan. Things happened to me that I took advantage of. I'm like the night driver who can't see beyond his headlights, yet is able to make a journey of hundreds of miles with that limitation.

The long and the short of it was that I agreed to try it. Doyle would make all the arrangements with the nuns, and I'd move in with him.

"I want a room of my own," I said to Doyle, too much aware of the congested conditions at the orphanage.

"You got it," he said, and showed me a broom closet of a room on the second floor up a narrow flight of stairs from the kitchen, obviously a room built into the attic at an earlier time. It held a spindle bed, a small dresser, a chair, a table, a coat rack, and an oleograph of the Sacred Heart, Jesus with the golden hair down to his shoulders, sad-eyed at the sins of the world.

"The guest room," he said, smirking. "Used to be mine when Mother was alive."

"It's okay," I said. I looked at the door. "Does it lock?"

"Christ, boy, you're in a house with relatives."

"So it doesn't lock?"

"And what in the name of God would the likes of you have that I'd want to steal?"

Flashing thoughts of my mother's talk about Doyle flitted in and out of my mind.

"All right," I said finally. "But...one thing..."

"What?"

"To make up for the drop in pay" — I stopped his interruption with a wave of my hand — "I know, I know. It's pay — and found. But I want one more thing — a chocolate bar of my choice every day."

He laughed, relieved at a condition that cost him little.

"Got a sweet tooth, have you?"

"I do."

"All right then — I've one myself — one chocolate bar a day."

And so it was settled. He spoke with Mother Superior, and I arranged with Joe Gallant for Billy Williams to take over my job at the dairy. The day I was to leave, Mother Superior called me in for a chat. I expected the usual exhortation to keep up my attendance at Sunday Mass, to attend to my religion, but it wasn't that at all.

"Michael," — she always called me that — "are you happy with this arrangement?"

"Yes, Mother."

"Your — ummm — relative isn't exerting any kind of pressure on you to do this?"

"No, Mother."

She studied me for a long few moments.

"Joe Gallant tells me you've developed into a responsible worker. Keep that up and you'll go far."

Her eyes softened, and she startled me with a quick hug. She was not generally a touching person.

"We'll miss you," she said. "But remember — if it doesn't work out you're more than welcome to return."

I nodded, feeling my eyes filling. In the space of a second, a parade of nuns went through my head: the tough and fair Superior; Sister Emily Alphonsus in the refectory, stern and angular but dispensing extra food and milk with a crinkling at the corners of her eyes; Sister Margaret Philip, the chubby and cheerful disciplinarian who teased and cajoled you into obedience and when that didn't work had not the heart for stern discipline but paraded offenders before Mother Superior for the tough love necessary; Sister Emily John, the old, bent housekeeper, always in the corridors, sweeping, polishing, praying, with a never-empty pocketful of peppermint "sweeties" that she dispensed liberally as she dispensed her love to all "my children."

"Thank you, Mother," I said. "For everything."

She nodded, her head half-turned, speaking gently over her shoulder. "There's a couple of your friends waiting out front to say goodbye."

So many of the momentous events in my life seem to have taken place in the fall of the year. I can smell the fragrance of fallen leaves on the crisp cool air, the westering sun throwing long shadows along the lane, and I see Emily Kate in her old plaid jacket with her hands thrust into the pockets waiting for me, trying to hide the look of betrayal in her eyes. Billy was there, too, hanging back, his face blank, wishing he was anyplace else.

Little was said. Emily Kate took one hand from her pocket and gripped my arm and told me I was lucky to have found a home. At that moment I almost changed my mind.

"I may never see you again," she said.

"Come on, Emily Kate. I'm only a couple of miles away. You can drop in any time you're in town."

She shook her head. "No. If you want to see me, you come visit me here."

"What's the difference?"

"If you don't understand that, then you've learned nothing."

It was mysterious to me, but I nodded emphatically, wanting her blessing even as I abandoned her, wanting her to think well of me, even then calculating in my head how I could appease her, keep her thinking well of me.

"Of course I'll come and see you."

She gave me a long look and a hug even quicker than Mother Superior's. She opened the door to go inside and looked back; I could see in her eyes, in the set of her mouth, that I was no longer a part of her world.

"No, you won't," she said, and slammed the door. Billy just looked at me. "Always thinking about yourself, ain't you?" he said, and followed after Emily Kate. There was no parting handshake, nothing.

I stood there on the porch, cold and alone, leaves swirling around my legs, doubting yet again the wisdom of my choice, the words of a new poet Emily Kate had introduced me to ringing in my ears: "In the lost boyhood of Judas, Christ was betrayed."

At last, my decision final, I groaned in self-pity, then picked up the small case that contained all I owned, and began trudging the familiar two miles down the road into Charlottetown.

CHAPTER 4

Life with Aloysius Doyle gave me experience in a new world. Where before I had been only the worker, I now began lessons in entrepreneurship, however minor and shabby the business. I was the purveyor of goods, mostly candy to children: the hardhats, the jawbreakers, the rolls of sweeties, the suckers, the old-fashioneds, the bubble gum — the penny purchases that allowed men like Aloysius Doyle to survive. There was also of course the odd five-cent sale of a chocolate bar or ten or twenty cents for a small or a large package of Turret or Sweet Caporal cigarettes, or a pack of Ogdens for the makings with the yellow Vogue or red Chanticleer cigarette papers. And we were not above selling cigarettes to kids either, for a penny each from a broken package kept under the counter for just such a purpose.

I knew that old Doyle was watching me closely in those early months, and I never cheated him out of a penny. I was aware that occasionally when he left me in charge he would walk around the block, climb the stairs to Lou McMahon's tailor shop across the street, and settle himself beside Lou's partner, Billy Morgan, on the table by the window where he had a clear view of his own front door; and when he returned and said, as he always did, "Anything doing?" I would faithfully report the number of customers and the nature and amount of their business.

But I, too, was a watcher, and when he emptied the till at night into a well-worn canvas bag, I would make a point of disappearing or at least being extremely busy as he took it to the stash he kept somewhere in the back — either in the kitchen or his bedroom off the kitchen. I made a wager with myself that it was the bedroom; that's where he'd keep it, I thought, so that anybody breaking in would have him to deal with, although I thought often as well that the take from penny candies, chocolate bars, and cigarettes would hold little temptation for any self-respecting thief.

I was in no hurry; I knew I'd discover his hide in plenty of time. I wasn't going anywhere — not yet, at any rate, and meanwhile I enjoyed another kind of freedom, the freedom to wander around the city.

Not far away, down next door to Rix's Grocery at the corner of Kent and Queen, was a store similar to Doyle's, but run by kindly old P. J. McCloskey. In all the years I knew him, I never knew what the P. J. stood for, probably Patrick James or something like that; he was of the Irish County Monaghan people who'd settled here in an area called Emyvale named after their own village in Ireland. I often dropped into his place for a glass of buttermilk at his counter, and didn't have to worry about his Christian name since he was always "Mr. McCloskey" to me, a thin, bespectacled man but always with a kind word and a ready smile. His son, Art, was called "Pickle," and his daughter's name was Katherine, both of them older, both of them with the old man's kindly traits. Myrtle Semple worked in the store part-time, an "older woman" — maybe eighteen or so — with whom all the youngsters were in love. Mrs. McCloskey appeared from time to time; this was very much a family business.

It got so I spent a lot of my spare time in there chatting up Myrtle and Mr. McCloskey, learning, through him, matters about business that I should have been learning from Doyle. The simple matter of haggling with the wholesalers to save money, for instance, was something unknown to me. Doyle never did it that I knew of, and when I mentioned it to him one night as he was paying bills, papers scattered all over the kitchen table, he drew back and stared down at me a moment, eyes narrowed, smoke dribbling from his nostrils, the ashtray at his elbow overflowing.

"Don't go getting ideas above yourself."

"I'm not. I just thought —"

"Let me do the thinking around here. Bargaining, is it? By Jesus, if I could ever get even with Carvell's, I might be able to think of it. But why should I? They carry me, they done it for years."

"Yes, but if you offered them—"

"Forget it, boy." Then, suspicious, "You been talking to someone?"

"No."

"Well, don't. You don't need to worry about being a businessman."

"I'm not."

From which I inferred that the old bastard had no intention of including me in his will, an eventuality that would have surprised me greatly anyway, for I knew he had nephews and nieces waiting in the wings for him to die.

✳

One day, about three months after I began working for him, old Doyle walked in the door of the shop just as I popped a hardhat into my mouth. He glared at me.

"Eating the profits," he said, and banged me on the head.

"I put my penny in the till," I shouted.

He grabbed me and the gust of moonshine in my face almost made me puke.

"Don't lip me, boy." He gave me another crack, and I ended up under the counter wiping the blood from my face. He stood over me breathing heavily, then stormed out, and I knew he was headed back for more courage. I removed my penny from the till and shoved it back in my pocket. "To hell with you," I muttered through my puffed lip and the handful of hardhats I crammed in my mouth.

I was in bed when I heard him stumbling around in the

store muttering to himself. There was silence for a while, then I heard him on the stairs.

"Are you awake, Mickey?"

"I'm awake."

The light seeping up from below showed him weaving in the doorway.

"Here. I brought you up a couple of bars of chocolate."

"I already had my bar for the day."

"These are extra, you know, for...ummm...."

"It's okay. I don't want them."

His voice roughened. "You'll take them."

"Okay."

"There's no need to hold a grudge," he said.

He made me sit up and eat the chocolate bars, but worse, he made me listen to his drunken ramblings and croaking songs for hours before he fell into a drunken sleep across the foot of my bed after nibbling half the night on a bottle of rum which now lay empty on the floor. I finally drifted off to his stentorian snoring, and when I awoke in the morning he was gone.

I couldn't have this, I decided, I needed my sleep, so the next day I got Mr. Ford in the blacksmith shop across the street to make me a metal wedge, which I banged securely under the door each night, held from sliding by a nail I drove into the floor.

The next time Doyle came to my room, he kicked and thrust at the door. I thought it would break as it held securely at the bottom but bent inwards at the top. I pushed against it, bracing it, and he must have known I was just inside as he wheedled and begged.

"C'mon, Mickey, open the door. I have some bars for you. You know I'm good to you, that I love you like a son."

I put my back to the door, my hands over my ears. It was too humiliating, and I wiggled my fingers in my ears to drown out his voice. Finally, he gave the door a kick, and I heard him curse loudly, and then the stairs creaked as he left. The next morning nothing was said, but I knew he'd be looking in my room for the wedge so I'd put it in a cotton bag and hung it from a nail under the sill outside my window. He never did find it.

I laid traps for him and discovered he was often in my room: my few socks or underwear in different positions, the bedclothes shifted, the chair or dresser moved. It must have driven him mad. I even strengthened the holding power of the door by working a hole in the top casing to take a four-inch spike, tapping it home each night with the heel of my shoe, shoving it into the bag with the wedge each morning. Eventually the searches stopped and I guessed he figured I took the wedge with me each day in my pants pocket, or else he was being as foxy as myself in rearranging my belongings.

The beatings, the rough treatment, only got worse. I don't know how many times he came into the store barking at me.

"How much did you steal today?"

"Nothing."

"Oh yeah? Empty your pockets."

I submitted to this shameful treatment a few times until I started keeping nothing in my pockets, and leaving them inside-out when I saw him coming in a foul mood. The next time he demanded I turn out my pockets, I just held my hands away from my sides.

"Smart young bastard," he snarled, and whacked me anyway.

And there were occasions when I was out back that I heard him with certain women being oily and sly.

"Small pack of Sweet Caps, Aloysius."

"Ten cents," he said. There was a slight pause, and he gave a kind of sick laugh.

"Tell you what," he said. "Keep your dime. Maybe you and I can work something out."

"Oh? Like what?"

"Like maybe you could come in and see me later. I'll send the boy to bed."

"You expect a lot for ten cents."

"Well, howbe if you had free cigarettes for a week?"

"Howbe a month?"

"Well — okay, a month."

"You old rip," she snorted. "I don't think I could stand to be near you if you supplied me with cigarettes for a year. Here's your dime."

There was a tinkle of a coin on the glass case, then a slamming door and the loud jingling of the bell over it.

After such rebuffs, it was not safe for me to open my mouth. In fact, I usually disappeared quietly upstairs in case he'd suspect I'd heard any of the exchange.

But they weren't all rebuffs, and I learned another side of business — that if the price is right, you can often get what you want.

I thought of my mother working in this kind of place — how many years ago? — and my stomach dropped at the thought that old Doyle might even be my father. I looked for signs of myself in him, and found none. But the thought, the possibility, lingered and would not leave me. For me, this was just further ammunition to stoke my hatred and to add to my battle plan against Doyle, a plan for revenge that was slowly forming in my imagination.

The knockings at my door did not cease for a year, but he finally gave up. Anytime he came near me in the store, I shied away, my distaste evident, and he never quite knew how to deal with it.

I watched him warily, my hatred growing and growing. Just wait, you old bastard, I thought often, just wait, I'll get even. It was that thought, that hatred, that kept me there. That, plus the fact that I had no place to go except the orphanage, but I viewed return there as failure, and I would not admit that. Every time I thought of the orphanage, my stomach flipped. Emily Kate had been right again — I did not go back to see her, even though each time I thought of her I vowed anew that I would. But I never did. I was only too aware that out on the edges of town were our penal institutions, our jail, our orphanages, our insane asylum. They were a sort of outer ring, a warning, a last line for those of us who threatened to spin out of control, and I feared them all.

✻

In keeping with the custom of the day, Queen Square School was an all-boys Catholic school, and a right shifty bunch of young ruffians we were. I was by now in Madelyn Clarkin's Grade Five class. Some of the guys in her class included Ivan Docherty, Harrison Ryan (who for some reason related to a history class was nicknamed after the British pretender Perkin Warbeck), Duck MacDonald, Dagger DeCoste, Moe Goodwin, Nails Dowling, Turtle Tulle, Big Louie MacDonald, and Triffle Martin, who earlier had gone by the undignified name of Shrimp until he was offered some jam one day in the soup kitchen and said, "I'll have just a trifle," mispronouncing it "triffle," and the name stuck.

None of us was much of a fighter, except Ivan who was tough and actually fought later in the ring for a couple of years until he discovered easier ways to make a living; and Big Louie who, because of his size, never had to fight anyway. The rest of us got picked on regularly in the playground by the older boys; one who seemed destined to make my life miserable was Bumble Flynn — bigger, but not that much bigger, like a bulldog, so sure of himself that he often had the battle won before it began. He would bluster and bluff and opponents like myself would back down. I went out of my way to avoid him.

Big Louie watched this shameful performance for some weeks, then one day hauled me over by the chestnut tree at the edge of the playground. "Look," he said, "are you going to spend your life running away from Bumble Flynn?"

I was no hero. "If I have to."

"But you don't. The way you deal with a bully like that is head on."

"Easy for you to say — you're big enough."

"It's got nothing to do with size. It's all in attitude and surprise. Here, let me show you."

For the next few days, Big Louie, who sat just behind me in class, showed me the basic moves in boxing and kept whispering over and over in my ear, "You can beat the shit out of him." The words "positive reinforcement" would have meant nothing to him — or to me — but he knew instinctively that what I needed was belief in myself.

Sooner than I wished, the opportunity came to test my so-called self-confidence. In secret moments of doubt, which came often, I felt that each day was a ceremony to my helplessness, incident following incident, especially marked for my humiliation. Opposing this was the soothing voice of Big Louie which displayed more confidence in me than I ever could in myself.

When the moment came, it arrived with a suddenness that surprised me; I had no time to think about the possible outcome, of being afraid, of being made appear a coward.

"Here he comes," Big Louie said. "Remember what I told you."

The preliminaries took only seconds. I was baited, accused of ducking him, of being yellow. This was the ultimate boyhood insult, the one that demanded action: challenge or run.

"Let's go into the *Patriot* yard and settle it," I said.

The backyard of the *Patriot* — the evening newspaper — bordered on the back of the school out of sight of teachers. It was the place where arguments were settled, where not a few noses were broken and eyes blackened. Over several generations, it was the place where enough tears were spilled by Queen Square boys in humiliation, frustration, anger, and fear to float the *Queen Mary*, and the number of "fucks" murmured, spoken, shouted, or rammed down throats would easily exceed the number of words in the average dictionary. The *Patriot* yard was the jousting arena, the ring, the Roman amphitheatre for Queen Square School. It was the place where reputations were made — and destroyed. It was a dirty, scraggly back lot, but it was the supreme testing ground for those Queen Square boys aspiring to a dignified manhood. The young and innocent fought for "King of the Castle" on the cellar hatches on the schoolyard side of the building, but out here, on the other side of the new wing, authentic life was lived, the real business of school took place, personalities were formed and character traits developed that became associated with the participants for life.

When I rose to his challenge, Bumble Flynn was surprised at my reaction, and I thought I detected a faint glimmer of uncertainty. I clung to that thought as we trudged around the building surrounded by a noisy, jostling crowd of high-spirited onlookers eagerly anticipating the spilling of any blood other than their own. They formed a loose ring around us. Bumble thrust his snarling face at me, bunching my sweater in his fist.

"Tough guy, eh? You're nothing but a yellowbelly."

My mind went blank, and I pushed him away and swung wildly with my left. I actually saw his nose bend sideways as blood spurted. I moved in close then and kneed him in the groin, and as he came forward I chopped down with my right hand into the bloody mess of his face, dimly aware of his screaming as he fell to the ground, hands to his face, curling himself into a fetal position.

I knew how Wyatt Earp felt at the OK Corral. I stood over him for a few moments to be sure it was over then reached down and wiped my bloody hands on his jacket, kicked him once in the gut, and turned away, my face showing nothing, my eyes straight ahead, ignoring the shouts of glee of those always willing to see a bully get his comeuppance, ignoring the pats on the back, heading back to the schoolyard and into my classroom, where I found that word of my victory had preceded me.

The plan of attack had been Big Louie's, but the other touches — like the strutting — were my own. On my victory walk I acknowledged with a wink and a nod Big Louie's dirty-fighting instructions — hit first and hit hard and to hell with the Marquis of Queensbury — but I hugged within myself the knowledge that the aptitude had been mine. I was not only good at violence, but to my surprise I found that I liked it. I had discovered within myself the double personality engendered by school: the attentive boy in class, the unleashed cutthroat in the schoolyard.

CHAPTER 5

The third factor in my education — the joy of revenge — was a little longer coming my way, but a fourth characteristic — patience — developed somewhere during the journey, gave me the certain knowledge that revenge would come, that I would make it come, that it was only a matter of time.

I now knew for certain that old Doyle kept his stash in his bedroom. Many nights I covertly observed him as he dumped the cash from the till into his canvas bag and went into the kitchen, closing the door behind him, pausing there to rattle some dishes as if moving them to get at his hide, followed by silence except for the odd squeak of the floorboards as he slid into his bedroom to his real hiding place. One night I waited, crept to the kitchen door, poked it open with a finger, saw the room was empty, pulled the door back, then resumed reading at the counter.

"Is the front door locked?" he called presently from the kitchen.

"It's locked."

"Put out the lights then. Do your reading in here."

He'd been sober this time for about six months, since February, but I could tell he was working himself up for a breakout. He was edgy, critical, nervous, walking on eggs. I gave him a wide berth during those days, knowing that soon he'd turn magnanimous once he'd made up his mind to drink. He'd not act immediately. He'd usually hold off to begin on a Friday night, delay it, teasing and tempting himself for a few more days but already enjoying it.

When he took pains dressing going out on Friday, I knew this was the night. Even though I've done it myself, it never fails to amuse me when drinkers don their best bib and tucker to go out to get pissed, to slop drinks over themselves, to puke and fall down and come home looking and smelling like an abbatoir reject. Is it, perhaps, that we think this time will be different, this time we'll behave like gentlemen; this time, since we are presenting ourselves well-turned-out, we'll behave like moderate drinkers, just having a good time, stopping after the glow of the first few drinks has released our inhibitions?

How come the true drinker never learns, never gives up trying to retain that state of well-being, but always passes through it to insensibility, following the treacherous instinct which dictates that if six drinks make one feel this good, nine will prolong the feeling, never accepting that there is a cumulative effect to alcohol, leading far past well-being into stupidity, hangover, and remorse?

Ah well, bless old Doyle for never learning. When he left the house all dolled up that Friday night I knew he wouldn't be home early, if at all; he occasionally spent the night in a bootlegger's where they'd lay him out on a couch and throw a blanket over him for the night.

But, cautious, I did what I'd done a few times already: locked up and followed him down Queen Street to King and along past Pownal, noting in passing that Peter Hogan's store was still open while we were closed. But, then, he carried groceries, and there were more after-hour demands on stores like his.

When Doyle knocked and was admitted to a house, I leaned against the fence across the street and smoked four cigarettes over the next hour; then, satisfied that he was settled, I went back to the store, let myself in without turning on any lights, and went through into his bedroom where I closed the door and slid off the catch on the window before turning on the light. If I heard him at the front door I could be out the window in a matter of seconds; I knew because I'd done it. I'd oiled the window catch so that it slid easily back and forth, and I could work it from the outside with my pocket knife. Doyle would never notice, since he never opened the window or the blind, winter or summer. This, after all, was his vault.

In my mind I'd already eliminated the usual places: the drawers of his dresser, under the mattress, the clothes closet, although I held it in reserve; if I couldn't locate the hide fairly quickly, then it must be in the closet.

The ceiling — no — plaster. The walls the same. A quick glance under the bed for a strongbox — nothing but balls of dust. Now we were getting down to it. The floor, linoleum covered, a mat beside the bed. I lifted the mat — nothing. I got down on my hands and knees and quartered the room but found no slit of any kind in the lino. At last, I turned to the place I was saving in my mind, the place I would have chosen myself: the moulding around the base of the walls.

I found it behind the chair over which a sweater was carelessly draped, effectively covering it. It was well-hidden anyway, the narrowest of mitred cuts, a section of moulding about a foot in length, held in place by a single tiny screw. On top of the dresser I found the nailfile he'd use as a screwdriver, and I quickly removed the section. Inside was a hollowed-out space stretching on either side of the opening and into which were crammed several canvas bags. I poked them, jamming my fingers on a couple crammed with hard coins, but feeling for those on the sides that gave off the soft rustle of paper. Making sure I disturbed nothing, I quickly replaced the section of moulding, the chair and sweater, and the nailfile. I refastened the window catch, turned off the light, let myself out the door, closed it and crept upstairs to my own room to lie on the bed, smoking, gloating.

The wheels of my revenge had started turning. All I had to do was wait.

I hung out around Gump McMahon's poolroom on Grafton Street and George Tulle's Charlottetown Alleys in the basement of the Market Building. Bowling and pool and billiards and snooker did not then have the uptown reputation they have today when you see modern leather-chaired emporia aimed at attracting not only the upwardly mobile but women as well. Ah, equality. Then, a pool hall, if not a den of iniquity, was at least a hangout for ne'er-do-wells, those expected to amount to nothing, the school truants and dropouts, those generally with no future. The Holy Name Club on Richmond Street, a hangout for some of the Queen Square School boys, was thought to be less rowdy than the others, perhaps by virtue of its name and its Catholic attachment, but it seemed to me that every bit as much smoking, drinking, cursing, and blasphemy went on there as elsewhere, although manager Gordon Essery ran a tight ship and tried to keep the lid on as much as possible.

It was at the Charlottetown Alleys I spent most of my spare time, bowling now and then, but mostly working on my billiard game. I took note of the smooth silent confidence that exuded from Bill Nicholson and Duck Acorn when they shot, the sense of having it all together, and I emulated them as I worked at erasing all feeling from my eyes and face, showing the world nothing. I needed self-control, mastery, so I would never betray myself.

How did I know all this at such an early age? I look back today at kids who are now the age I was then, and search their faces closely. Are they doing what I was doing then, plotting, scheming, conspiring — wearing an innocent air, smiling at an unsuspecting world? Now and again, I will note their eyes change, but I tell myself that this is just a natural reaction, the crossness you can spot even in the face of an infant when he doesn't get his way. No, I convince myself, I was unusual that way, I had insight beyond my years, the gift of survival, forced on me by an uncaring world. Had I been one of the young Jews forced to march hundreds of miles across a barren Europe to freedom back in the thirties, I would have made it.

The alleys were a hangout for many West-Enders, and it was here that I once again encountered Frankie Hanlan. Taller, tougher, handsomer than ever, cocky, brash — that would just about describe the Frankie of those years. He had a part-time job working on Tom Power's delivery jigger, mostly humping cartons from warehouse to jigger, from jigger to store. Knowing Frankie of the swift hands, I knew he was also making plenty on the side, both from DeBlois Brothers, for whom Tom Power hauled, and from the various stores as well. I often saw him in the dark area to the right as you entered the alleys, the place where shady deals were completed, goods exchanged — Frankie gesturing, smiling, trading, selling. I envied him. He had time for me, but it was the big brother routine, a poke in the ribs, a rustle of the hair, a pat on the cheek. I wanted to impress him, to have him treat me as an equal, but that didn't seem likely to happen.

Frankie was always running a comb through his curls, shaping them with his hands, preening before any shop window that offered a reflection. His hero in those days was the flashy Legs Diamond, a big-time flamboyant gangster of a few years earlier, a man who'd been shot on four separate occasions, and survived each time, a tall, handsome, charismatic leader who could charm the hardest heart. Unfortunately for Legs, the fifth attempt on his life succeeded, when, on 18 December 1931, two assassins put three bullets in his head in the early hours of the morning as he slept off a victory celebration after being acquitted on a kidnapping charge of an uncooperative moonshine trucker.

Frankie would extol Diamond's feats, having read about

him in *True Detective,* or some other pulp magazine, to us his ardent audience. "Legs was sure he'd been ratted out on the earlier attempts," Frankie said, "and he hated a squealer. He never squealed himself even when it could have helped him, and he shot one of his own men when he tried to sell him out."

Frankie would look wise and say, "No, boys, I tell you, there ain't nothing worse than a squealer. Legs said once, 'Even God hates a squealer,' and that's the truth." Frankie'd look menacing and growl, "So don't let me hear of any of youse guys giving me up to the cops."

✳

As more and more of my real life seemed to be unfolding at the bowling alleys, it became harder and harder to face work in the shop and go "home." Then one night old Doyle triggered an event that was to change my life. He came in plastered and staggered into the kitchen before I could get up the stairs to my room. I started past him, and he lashed out, catching me on the side of the head. I lay in the corner by the stove, groggy, covering up as he kicked at me, his hard-toed boots bruising my ribs and thighs. He kicked and missed and stumbled in his drunkenness, and I rolled under the table and out the other side, came swiftly to my feet, grabbed the heavy water pitcher off the table, and belted him on the head with it. He collapsed, groaning, clutched his head, still conscious. I debated hitting him again, but didn't, standing there, poised, as he slowly shook his head, clearing it.

"Don't you ever lay a finger on me again," I said. I didn't need to act. "The next time I'll kill you."

He took his time, sobering, licking his lips, sizing me up. He pulled himself to his feet supported by the table, finally standing erect, weaving only slightly. I could follow his thought processes, moving from outrage, to speculation, to caution, to something akin to fear, to slyness.

"So this's the thanks I get after all I done for you."

"I earned my keep."

"And now it's over, boy. I want you out of here first thing in the morning."

"I was leaving anyway. You couldn't beg me to stay."

He laughed. "You don't fool me, boy. You'd stay as long as you got a free ride."

"Nothing was ever free with you, Doyle."

I thought I'd gone too far, and as his eyes hardened I tightened my grip on the pitcher, hefting it, sneering at him, defying him. It worked, and he subsided, laughed again a bit shakily, and wheeled out of the kitchen.

"Be gone in the morning," he threw back over his shoulder, stopping to empty the till into his pocket, slamming the front door, the bell over it jangling for a full ten seconds as he headed back to the protection of his booze.

I went up to my room and, as a matter of habit, even though I was certain old Doyle wouldn't be home tonight, jammed in my wedge and spike, then, at peace with what I was planning to do, climbed into bed and slept soundly.

CHAPTER 7

The next morning, Saturday, I pulled my old suitcase from under the bed and packed my few clothes. I'd gambled that Doyle wouldn't return, and when I checked, his bedroom was empty.

I brought out the needle I used to sew on buttons and repair clothing, a whittled-down popsicle stick that I'd honed to a sharp tip the night before, and took down Doyle's bowl of soft-centre candy from the kitchen shelf. I got the tube of rat poison from the back porch and went to work. In fifteen minutes I was finished.

I replaced the candy on the shelf, and left everything neat and clean, a hell of a lot cleaner than when I first came. Doyle could not fault me in that regard, although I was well aware that the word on me would be on the street. But then everyone knew what a mouth he had, and the general feeling, I believed, was that I was a pretty good kid who had to put up with a lot, and further — and this counted with the crowd that mattered to me — I was one who knew how to keep his mouth shut.

My very first problem was finding a place to stay, but what I'd said to him about thinking of leaving was true. One day in the alleys, I'd talked about it with Frankie, and he'd told me of the place he was staying, a rooming house on Dorchester Street. He knew there were vacancies because the old lady was always growling about how she needed more boarders to make any money. I found it with a "Rooms to Let" sign in the window, and, when I knocked, the door was opened by a squinty-eyed old lady who stood about five feet tall and easily would have topped 200 pounds. She introduced herself as Mrs. Emily Dunn, "a widow woman," and, yes, she had a room for five dollars a week — six with breakfast — and would I like to see it. I would, and when I said it was fine she asked how I'd be paying. I gave her twenty-four dollars for a month in advance — with breakfast — and her eyes lit up. "You're my kind of boarder," she said, and I knew I had an ally.

For the remainder of the weekend I ventured out rarely and only where I'd be seen: as far as the alleys for a couple of hours on Saturday, to Percy Vail's or the New England Café for something to eat, to Duffy's for some candy. I hung out a bit around the corner of Dorchester and Queen with the usual gang, spitting, cursing, sniffing, stamping our feet, wondering when the Mounties and City cops might organize their next raid and, in the meantime, if Bill or Lal LeBlanc might have a spare drop of corn whiskey, laughing when Bill replied in his fast mutter, "Nothing in boys, nothing in," and Lal added, chuckling, "Only a drop for ourselves," knowing that Bill, who had been Don Messer's first drummer and still loved to get a session going in his kitchen, would later relent and invite everybody back up the street for a quick noggin or two. They were a great gang around that corner; many of them went into the services over the next year or so and not all of them returned after the war.

They'd had the word about me, and when someone said, "Too bad that old bastard kicked you out," I merely shrugged and said I was getting ready to leave anyway, and it could be the best thing that ever happened to me, since it would force me to look around for something to do. I didn't begin at once to hang around Frankie, since there were too many weights tied to me that I wished to shed before I became close with anyone. I knew that eventually my ingratiating way would win him over; Frankie needed an acolyte, an admirer, some- one to lead the applause, and I elected myself to the role.

Sunday night after dark I told Mrs. Dunn I was going up

to White's Restaurant for a bite to eat. Once I rounded the corner to Queen Street I began to run, slowing as I got to Hughes's corner. I slipped into the gangway next to Wellner's Jewellers which took me into the common backyard for many of the businesses in the area, including Doyle's. I went to the back window, listened carefully but could hear nothing. I slid the blade of my penknife between the windows and pushed back the catch without a sound just as I'd practised a hundred times. I eased the window up and peeked around the blind, seeing nothing. I climbed in, noting the sour smell, letting my eyes adjust to the dark, then opened the bedroom door slowly to the sight of old Doyle flat on his back on the floor of the dining room, puke all over him, dead. The bowl of candy was still on the table, four remaining in it. I dumped them into a dishcloth, and stuffed the works in my jacket pocket, wiped the bowl inside and out and placed it back on the sideboard. Like a shadow, I slipped into the bedroom, out the window, refastened the clasp, out the gangway, a quick peek, then up and around the corner to White's Restaurant, the whole operation taking no more than five minutes. I made a point of jollying up the waitress, one of the cute blonde MacDonald sisters from out Dundee way, ate a Western sandwich and a glass of milk and a piece of cream pie, and went straight back to Mrs. Dunn's, stopping for ten seconds at the street grate at the Bank of Nova Scotia corner to jam the rag and the candy down into the sewer.

The police came Monday afternoon about one o'clock, a Sergeant and a Constable. They wished to see me, and I was appropriately mystified. They told me Mr. Doyle was dead — a heart attack apparently — and they wished to notify me as a relative, but they also wished to ask a few questions. When they asked if we got along, I said we got along okay until last Friday, and I told them everything, including how I'd hit him with the pitcher. They nodded, and I knew they already knew about it. They asked me about my weekend activities, and I told them the few places I'd been and, oh yes, I was up to White's Restaurant last evening for a lunch, and that's the farthest I've been away from the house here. It was quite a shock getting thrown out, you know, and I have to think about what I'm going to do. I've saved up a bit of money but that won't last forever. I'm really sorry to hear about Mr. Doyle because he was really a good man — they exchanged a quick glance — and even though we had our differences, he was kind to me, although he had this, you know, weakness, and drank too much at times, but who would have thought, at his age and all, not too old, a heart attack?

I was talking too much so I shut up, just sitting there shaking my head. They asked me about his money, and I told them vaguely that as far as I knew he kept it in the bank, he deposited each week, but he never let me in on his business affairs. I told them he'd emptied the till on Friday night when he'd stormed out after our fight. They came back to my trip to White's, but when they substantiated with Mrs. Dunn that I'd been gone less than an hour they dropped it. I knew they'd check with the restaurant, and I knew I'd be remembered.

It was too early yet to let my exhilaration show, and I had to sit hard on the explosion building inside me, the danger being, I felt, that I might implode. It was allowable, however, to pace my room and rain down muttered jubilant curses on the dear departed.

It made me feel better, but I won't pretend that the changes in my life over the next while were easy. The acceptance of what I'd done — it didn't all happen at once. For a long time, over a period of weeks, there seemed to be no passing time, no plan except for the moment. It was like living in the world of an eternal present where the moment, whether one of bright sunshine or darkest gloom, took on an aura, an added sheen, like living my life under a series of flashing bulbs, as if I were always on stage, even in the privacy of my room living the parts, speaking the dialogue, creating actions for my unseen audience. Passing a store window I would observe myself, adjusting my posture, neutralizing my expression, occasionally winking conspiritorially at my invisible fans. No feelings of horror or self-hatred or sorrow for what I'd done ever entered my soul. Fear was all, the fear of being caught.

I had two immediate problems: what to do about a job, and when to empty Doyle's stash. I'd left it when I'd found him dead for reasons of time, but mostly because I wanted no taint to adhere to me should someone know of it and say it was stolen. I didn't want it eventually found in my possession, as it would have been if I'd taken it to my room. I was fairly sure the secretive Doyle would have told no one, although I could easily see him in his cups bragging that he had enough set by to keep him. But this could refer to his bank balance, and I hoped he had a few extra dollars there to shift the police and greedy relatives away from any suspicions in my direction.

I'd gone to the funeral as one of the mourners, looking sufficiently hypocritical but getting the fish eye anyway from the assorted nephews and nieces. I kept to myself, wanting none of their company or their condescension. I didn't give a shit for any of them, so it was easy for me to parade through the ritual with my mind in neutral.

Then I sat back and waited. I had a visit from Leo O'Connell, Doyle's lawyer, who informed me in his jerky, rapid-fire manner, "The old man left you nothing, Mickey, miserable old bastard, and how are you getting on anyway, you must be finding it rough going, and I hope you get a job soon, and here's twenty to keep you afloat for a while," and he was out the door before I could thank him properly.

I waited a week and then decided to act. Someone else might discover the stash, or one of the relatives might move in and make it impossible for me to enter the building, or they might sell the property, or God knows what might happen. In my mind, that money was now rightfully mine, so I decided to go get it.

I had not been idle and had looked for and found a hiding place in the old cemetery on Elm Avenue. With a fence around it, protected by huge shade trees, and with rarely a visitor, it was a good place, but it was only when I fell over a downed stone into another, which gave a hollow ring when my fist struck it, that I understood what destiny meant. The hollow stone was painted to look like grey marble, but I scraped it with my pocket knife and found that it was metal, closer examination revealing a side panel screwed into place which some diligent work soon released to reveal the hollow inside. I looked around — nobody — so I hastily replaced the panel, noting its location under a white birch tree and the name "MacCallum."

At two in the morning I let myself quietly out of Mrs. Dunn's with a pillowcase stuffed inside my jacket. I had no trouble. I emptied Doyle's stash into the pillowcase by the light of a small pocket flash, replaced the moulding, and left, sneaking along the streets, on the far side from Ed's Taxi, the all-night dispatcher napping at his desk, my bag heavy on my shoulder, my ancient cap low on my head like an old rag-picker on the bum. In the cemetery, I knelt in the moon's narrow path, on top of the crusty, ice-covered grave of the poor Scottish crofter, the bare trees cracking in the spring breeze, the night air cold, moonlight glinting off the scattered money and the ghostly sentinels around me. Far from being afraid in these spectral surroundings, I was exulting. It was clear to me then that my ordained task in life was not to be afraid any longer, but, on the contrary, to be the one to induce fear in others.

Quickly now, I filled my pockets with coins, pleased to see that they were mostly dimes, quarters, and fifty-cent pieces, and I jammed a hundred dollars in bills on top of the coins. I'd count the rest another time. It was dry inside the grave marker; I shoved in the canvas bags, the coins on the bottom. Then I left, returning by another route, Prince to Dorchester — and home.

With money in hand, the matter of a job seemed unimportant, and it was, except for appearances. One could get by for a while flashing money with no visible means of support, but could not do it indefinitely. I knew how these things worked. All it would take would be one voiced suspicion which would lead to another which would then develop into a, "Do you suppose—?" which, inside a week, would be a confirmed rumour, "I got it from a guy who knows, he really found old Doyle's stash — they say he's got a fortune." The word would spread, get to the police as these things always do, and I'd have visitors again. No, I needed a job if only to protect myself. I had finished Grade Ten, my formal education was over, and now, at sixteen, it was time to get serious about work.

I tried Carvell's. No, they didn't need anyone but I might check with their truckers. I did, all except Tom Power for whom Frankie worked, and got chased by them all. I tried DeBlois Brothers with the same result. One of their drivers, encountered on Richmond Street, offered me a nickel to hold his horse while he nipped up Riley's Lane for a quick one, but I told him to jam his nickle, earning myself a flick of his whip across my neck, which smarted for two days.

I tried Peter Hogan's store, selling myself, emphasizing my experience, but Mr. Hogan smiled sadly and explained that he barely made enough for himself out of the business. I knew how well Doyle had done, so I doubted this, since Hogan also handled meat and groceries, but I couldn't call him a liar. I nodded understandingly, looking around his store, taking in the polished floor, the new mat inside the door, the clean shelves, the gleaming showcases.

"You keep a nice place, Mr. Hogan."

"It's work — all the time at something. Open till ten every night."

"I could take a lot of that load off you."

"Sorry, lad. No."

Okay, you old bastard, I said to myself with a patient smile. Pile it up, make bundles of it, and one of these fine days I'll come by and take it all from you.

CHAPTER 8

I began to be in and out of the offices of the *Patriot* on Richmond Street across from the alleys, next door to Reddin Brothers Drugstore. At the *Patriot* they were always in need of something: coffee, cigarettes, deliveries to various city sites, running copy to the CN Telegraph Office a few doors up the street. I picked up a few dimes — pocket money — for these insignificant jobs, but, more important to me than the money was the atmosphere around the newspaper office, the hustle and bustle as the paper was being prepared for press — the camaraderie, the banter among the writers, editors, and the back room gang, those responsible for the layout of the paper once the news had been written. It was here at the *Patriot* office that Leo O'Connell found me one day, giving me his fast talk about the possibility of a job.

"Now lookit here, Mickey, lookit here, the word is that they want a packing boy down at Fisher Brothers on Water Street, and if you get down there right away and ask for Alf McKearney and tell him I sent you, you just might get it. C'mon now, get off your arse. Get! Get!" And he shoved me out the door, grinning, dusting his hands, a job well-done. I liked Mr. O'Connell and his easy, friendly way. He had none of the standoffishness usually associated with lawyers, and when I said to him, "I'm going, Mr. O'Connell," he said, "Eh? Eh? Call me Leo, boy, call me Leo, everybody does."

The fix was in, I guess. Alf McKearney studied me around the smoke rising from his cigarette, a half-smile on his face.

"Leo tells me you're a good worker."

"I am."

"We'll see."

That was the job interview. The work entailed wheeling cases of tinned lobster on a hand truck from the long gleaming steel table where six girls sat, three on each side, labelling the cans as they came down the chute, sliding them along to the end where a couple of other girls packed them — twenty-four tins to a carton — another couple sealing them and setting them in piles of five on the floor.

It was my job — and Alf's — to truck each of the piles from this room to the large warehouse out back, or, on occasion, directly into a railroad car drawn up on a siding alongside the warehouse. It was continuous, back-breaking work just trying to do half as much as Alf McKearney, a bull of a man who could work for hours, pausing only occasionally for a few quick drags of a cigarette. He could be gruff if he thought you were goofing off, but he was ever mindful that others did not have his strength or energy, thus making it unnecessary to keep up with his unmerciful pace. I have witnessed many workers over the years, but I have yet to see anyone who could go head-to-head with Alf McKearney in his prime.

The noise on the floor was continuous: the rattle of the cans, the chatter of the girls, the teasing, the flirting. I began to feel their eyes on me. I was filling out, growing taller, no longer a skinny shrimp. With my quiet ways, my ready smile, I was vain enough to realize I was not a complete dog.

They teased me. "C'mon up and see me sometime, big boy." "How about giving a girl a break, Mickey?" "I'm free tonight, Mick." "Drop in anytime, Mick — as long as you're not too tired."

Oh, they laughed at me as I blushed under their teasing, their taunts, their innuendo, but it was good-natured laughter, and when I made my move on one of them, it was quiet little Mae Costello I approached, Mae who always smiled at me but did not take part in the rough banter.

"Why me?" she asked.

"Because I like you. You're quiet — like me."

"I don't know about you. You're going to be a heartbreaker."

"You mean I'm not already?"

We got along fine but had to undergo an unmerciful teasing when one of them spotted us together at a Saturday matinee at the Prince Edward. That soon died down, however, as we got to be accepted as a couple, always ignoring each other at work, barely even speaking. In fact, after we broke up, the others went a long time unaware of our split and would probably not have caught on at all if Mae had not come unstuck at work.

But that was later on. Oh, the girls had troubles, but the fatherly Alf let them vent as they saw necessary. His method of keeping the wheels turning was to ignore them. Their nimble fingers kept the cans flying — they never let up — but they could do this work and talk and chatter and cry and go on, the others filling in and working the harder if one of them took a few moments to weep. And he was wise enough to realize that when your people are working to capacity you do nothing to interrupt the rhythm, to inject anything as negative as criticism into what is now called the work environment. He believed, without ever putting it into words, that if it ain't broke you don't need to fix it.

❋

Nothing further was heard from the police about old Doyle, so one night after about a month I took another midnight trip to the cemetery to count the money. The total was $5,141.85, not a great amount by today's standards, but then more than two years' salary for the average working man. I lay back on poor MacCallum's grave — it was by now late April — gazing up at the stars thinking of faraway places. I was wealthy but I couldn't show it, I couldn't let anyone know I had money, or I'd be in deep trouble. I'd heard from Leo O'Connell about how disappointed Doyle's nephews and nieces had been at the small amount in his bank account, and how they were convinced there was more somewhere.

"What d'you think, Mickey, eh? Did he hide any of it away? Eh? Eh?"

"Not that I know of, Mr.— Leo. I never saw him hiding money or anything else. He wasn't a wealthy man. How much can you make on smokes and penny candy?"

"Yeah, yeah, I guess, I guess, and he did spend quite a bit on — when he went on a — well, you know, you know."

"That would explain it, wouldn't it?"

I didn't want anyone sniffing around me.

Since we were in the same rooming house, I now saw more and more of Frankie Hanlan, but it was still the elder-brotherly business, since Frankie had an aura about him that gave him a certain standing well above mine.

Most of his glamour resulted from the events surrounding his rum-running some time earlier. Still in his early twenties, he had already lived through more adventures than most men do in a lifetime. He basked in his reputation, and it was easy to imagine him in the part of rum-runner, the pleasant, smiling, eager-eyed Frankie, his blond curly locks dangling carelessly over one eye, the cigarette moving up and down as he spoke, definitely the air of a pirate about him. For months, he drank off the story of how his father's bootlegging contacts had landed him a job as crewman on the *Nellie J. Banks*, and his adventures under the great Newfoundland skipper, Captain Israel Lillington.

Frankie was a good storyteller, his laugh and gestures suggesting modesty, playing down his part, while at the same time subtly implying that his was really a major role.

"We was out of St. Pierre," he'd begin, "with a cargo of alcohol, Scotch, rum, gin, brandy, and about 20,000 smokes

— everything for sale. There was three Newfies in the crew, and me, and Captain Izzy — he was a Newfie, too. He was a pretty good drinker, I mean he drank every day, but, boy, could he handle a ship! And he liked to poke fun at the Mounties from outside the three-mile limit."

Frankie would pace around, eyeing each one in the audience, rubbing his hands, getting into it.

"We was coming down the west side of Cape Breton, past Cheticamp, and I had the middle watch." He'd pause and look questioningly at the faces around him, smoking, most of them, some with cynical smiles, most held by his tale.

"For any a youse landlubbers, that's from midnight to four a.m. Anyway, we passed Cape Breton, and I seen the East Point light fine on the starboard bow." He'd raise his right hand. "That's the right hand side, boys, for youse guys who ain't been to sea." And he'd laugh that infectious laugh that took any sting out of his words.

"So there we was in the early morning cruising along the north side of PEI, well outside the three-mile limit, when this goddam Mountie cutter fired a shot across our bow and forced us to heave to. Boy oh boy, was Captain Izzy mad. The Mounties came aboard and told us we was all under arrest, that just the day before Canada had set a new twelve-mile limit and we was inside it. Jesus, Captain Izzy went nuts. He hauled out his pistol and fired it into the deck like he was trying to sink the ship. By then, the Mounties had their guns out, too, but the Captain wasn't shooting at them. He was so goddam mad that he flung his gun as far as he could over the side. After he cooled down, he told the Mounties that he knew nothing about the new twelve-mile limit."

Frankie would pace again, hauling on a cigarette, shaking his head.

"The Mounties took us in tow to Charlottetown, and we lost the ship and the cargo. They threw us all in the clink, and, Christ, I can tell you we was thinking five or ten years, but after a coupla days they shipped the Newfies home and told me to get the hell out and stay away from rum-runners. Captain Izzy was let out on bail and went home, but came back for the trial in the spring."

Here, Frankie went all solemn and serious.

"The Captain had Jimmy Jones for a lawyer, and we all know he's the best around. Well, sir, Jimmy had the jury and the crowd almost in tears."

And here Frankie would pace up and down, thumbs hooked in an imaginary vest, giving his Jimmy Jones imitation.

"Gentlemen of the jury, I tell you the cruel RCMP are persecuting this man, this seafarer, who was merely cruising along the north shore of our beautiful Island, outside the three-mile limit, well within his rights to be carrying liquor and cigarettes, when the sneaky and treacherous federal government went and changed the law without so much as a friendly reminder to all respectable ship owners and captains."

You could tell that Frankie had this part memorized. He'd never have chosen such lofty language himself.

"This," he thundered, raising his right arm, shaking his fist, "this, gentlemen of the jury, is not good enough, not fair, not the way Canadians operate in an open and above-board honest way. This, gentlemen, is sly treachery, the work of sneaky bastards trying to screw honest workingmen carrying out their duties."

He dropped his arm. "Well, he didn't say 'bastards' or 'screw,' but that's what he meant." This usually brought a laugh and Frankie joined in and went on, "They tried to show how dangerous liquor was, but you could tell by the looks on the jury that they wasn't having any of that. The long and short of it was that they voted eight to four in the Captain's favour. But it wasn't done. The judge said they'd carry it over to the next session for a new trial."

Frankie turned gleeful. "But during the summer they decided to drop the case. They knew from experience that juries wouldn't convict rum-runners."

Frankie spread his hands to his audience. "The *Banks* was later sold by Customs, but neither Captain Izzy — or me — ever served a day in jail." He paused dramatically. "And that, gentlemen, is the great thing about Canadian justice — it pertects the innocent."

His uproarious laughter at this point usually mingled with that of his audience. It was a wonderful story, a kind of Robin Hood adventure, true for the most part, but polished and embellished by Frankie over time, until his modest part in the events reached the point where he became the central figure, the Captain's advisor and confidant, an accomplished navigator, a skillful ship handler, even a legal expert, suggesting strategies to Jimmy Jones which the latter was more than willing to implement. Like so many small-time crooks dreaming of glory, Frankie Hanlan pictured himself as Public Enemy Number One, but a generous man withal, admired by the public, conforming to his own vision of greatness.

✳

Life was good. I was at home in my job, beginning to get closer to Frankie, to absorb some of his magic, gaining more confidence, when one Friday Mae informed me that she'd missed her period for three months and was frantic.

"Well," I said, "what do you want me to do?"

"We could get married."

"Jesus, Mae, I'm not even old enough to join the Army."

"You were old enough to do this to me."

"Didn't you take any precautions?"

"Didn't you?"

This got us nowhere. I offered to pay for an abortion, but

Mae wouldn't hear of it.

"You know the Church don't allow it."

"To hell with the Church. It ain't the Church that's knocked up."

"No, Mickey, no. I'm going to have the baby."

"Okay, okay. We'll think of something."

I thought of something later that night, making a quick visit to the graveyard, and the next morning, Saturday, paying Mrs. Dunn three months in advance to hold my room, telling her I had family in Moncton who needed me for a while, and would she please call them at work on Monday and tell them I was called away. Then I got the bus to Wood Islands, crossed on the recently instituted Wood Islands-Caribou run, then into Pictou, staying overnight at the Stanley Hotel, then the next morning on to Halifax.

Before leaving, I'd called the orphanage.

"Sister, it's me — Mickey."

"Michael, is it yourself? I thought you must be dead."

"Yeah, I'm sorry, Sister. I shoulda called."

"Let me guess — you'd like to speak to Emily Kate?"

"If it's not too much trouble."

"You just hold on a minute, my boy, and I'll get her." I knew Emily Kate was still at the orphanage, teaching now in the school there, helping out with the young ones.

It was a long two minutes before she came on the line. I almost hung up a dozen times. Only the fact that I'd given my name to the Superior stopped me.

Emily Kate sounded breathless. "Yes, hello. Mickey?"

"Yeah, it's me."

"It's nice to hear your voice again."

"Good to hear yours, too."

"Why are you calling?"

"Can't I just call to be friendly?"

She laughed. "Sure. But it took you long enough."

"I know. I'm sorry. I was, uh, doing things."

"It doesn't matter. You're calling now. Are you coming out?"

"No. I, uh, have to go away for a few months, so I just called to say goodbye — for now."

"Why do you have to go away?"

"I just have to. Look, Emily Kate, you'll hear things about me. Don't believe everything."

There was a long pause. "What are you up to, for God's sake?"

"Nothing. Look, I gotta go. I just wanted to let you know."

"You never called before."

"I know. But I always felt you were close by, and I could reach out any time I wanted."

"But you never did."

"It's not too late, is it?"

"No, Mickey, it's not too late."

"That's all I wanted to know. Goodbye, Emily Kate. For now."

"Goodbye, Mickey."

When I hung up I was in a lather of sweat.

※

I'd heard Skinny Gallant and Ike McCabe talking about the Merchant Navy, so I already knew about the Merchant Seamen's Hut on Hollis Street; I went there, telling them I was between ships, and they put me up. I did look for a ship, visiting all the shipping offices along the waterfront, but they all had the same story — you had to be a member of the union. I didn't want to get that involved, and the stories I heard of exploding tankers, of survivors left drifting — as I huddled inside my double-tiered wire cubicle, three men I knew nothing about in the same space with me, my wallet hidden in my underwear — were enough to kill any desire to run away to sea. After a week I checked out, took the bus back to Pictou and had no trouble getting a job on the slip at the Ferguson Brothers Shipyard and a room in one of the staff houses on the outskirts of town.

I did nothing for the rest of the summer except work, read, go to the movies. Wartime allowed seven days of work if you wished, and most did since you were paid time-and-a-half on Saturdays, double-time on Sundays. It meant over a hundred dollars a week clear after room and board was deducted, a good deal of money at the time. I'd been in touch with no one at home, but there were several Islanders working here, and some of them nodded in recognition when we crossed paths on the job or in the big dining hall. Sooner or later word about me would filter back home, but I hoped to make a move of some kind before anyone came for me, if indeed anyone did. Mae had a couple of older brothers with nasty reputations, but I couldn't picture them making a special trip to Pictou to inveigle me into marrying Mae; if they came, they'd have my destruction in mind.

It didn't matter anyway because in October, after only three months in Pictou, I decided to return home.

CHAPTER 9

Since I am a newspaperman, it seems appropriate to write my story. The question facing me is how extensive a record of my darker nature I wish to make.

I begin: My life has been reduced to essentials. I eat, sleep, breathe, and grieve, finding — thanks to Eliot and Beckett — time present in time past, time future in time present, but all time rank with the rot of my life. The world is weary, the trees droop, the wind halts, the tides ebb and flow with an indifference matching my own, even the sunshine which my body craves is faded, dirty, lacking the lightness I remember.

That is crap. All that is crap, window dressing, showing nothing but depression and a bit of imitative flair. If I am a dirty old man with rotten memories, with a rotting body, so be it. Never let self-pity intrude: the code I've tried to live by.

I've tried so many times to concentrate my mind, but find it difficult even while passing inanities — especially when passing inanities. I'm interviewing someone over lunch, discussing the inner workings of government, who has the power, who's getting shafted, who's sleeping with whom, and at the same time I'm noting the details of his face, the way his mouth moves, the wateriness of his eyes, the colour of his necktie and if it matches his apparel, that awful chunk of red meat on his plate ready to gallop away. Meanwhile, I'm still admiring the ass on the new waitress, thinking how like little Theresa's it is, little untouchable Theresa who wiggled around for years in Ment's Restaurant; then, while coherently answering a question from my lunch partner, wandering off in my mind to the golf course, replaying the eighteenth hole, wishing I'd used a nine iron for the approach instead of a seven and ending up in the parking lot; I'm recording the laughter from the next table, the rattle of a broken muffler on a passing car, the clatter of dishes, the girl by the window putting on lipstick, the garlicky aroma wafting from the passing tray of escargot, the cooling bitter coffee, through it all knowing that the person opposite me has no idea of these multitudinous impressions. We all have similar experiences, it's just that so few people take note of what's happening to them from moment to moment.

It's impossible to do nothing, I have concluded. It is impossible to sit absolutely still and do nothing; there is always something happening in the mind. Or is that true? Is it not the aim of those who meditate to do just that — think of nothing, empty the mind — attaining after months, maybe years, of practice, what they call the state of nirvana — the moment when the mind becomes one with the Supreme Being? But is that doing nothing? No, I would submit, M'Lord, that that is the greatest activity and that nothing could be more active.

Henry James had the words for it: the atmosphere of the mind, and I wished mine to take on the nature of the wandering Bloom's, neither a *tabula rasa* nor a photographic plate, but a motion picture, ingeniously cut, carefully edited to emphasize the close-ups and fade-outs of flickering emotion, the angles of observation, the flashbacks of reminiscence.

How does one record, word by word, such symphonic material where certain instruments are heard, but where the voices of others are continually intruding? How keep the core of thought disengaged from the minutiae of the fringes? It cannot be done, and if it could it would tax our attention far beyond its capacity. The writer who tries it is too likely to create a text that's like a record of the noises at a hockey game, or of the self-recordings we all experimented with at parties when tape recorders were a novelty, the ensuing cacophony nothing but a blur of sound all but incomprehensible…. You expose a mind at the very moment it is thinking, and you challenge the reader to penetrate within it, but he will know only as much as this mind reveals.

During this time, as well, I was spreading my wings, engrossed in the maturation process. I suffered mentally and spiritually — but not much — after an experiment — may I call it that? — with the Sampson sisters. There was Glenda and her sister Sally, both of them pretty and vivacious, that summer living a carefree and casual life with their mother out at the old airport in huts that had been converted into apartments after the war. Their father had left or was dead, I don't remember; he wasn't there. At one time or another in that bright season, I was involved with both of them, ending up a little disgusted with myself but also with a sense of sneaky pride. Those happy, laughing girls moved away in the fall, and the event soon passed into the realm of memory.

> *Was it a year or lives ago*
> *We took the grasses in our hands*
> *And caught that summer flying low*
> *Over the waving meadow lands*
> *And held it there between our hands?*

Happiness? That's a word I have put under the microscope from time to time, but I found that it never held its shape. A meaning then, a purpose? The past, looked back on in this frame of mind, seems enveloped in something like a mist, something extraneous to the experience of it. I'm not talking about the poisoned itch of nostalgia, or the remorse, the regret. It's the moment when a word is spoken during a casual conversation and suddenly there is a click in our mind, a synapse is joined, and we say, "That's it, of course. I've known that, but I've never heard it put into words." Revelation. Discovery. There was damn-all of that in respect to the Sampson sisters.

I have spent my life seeking models, but have never been satisfied with the results. Should one look to the introspective Hamlet, the lovelorn Romeo, the sexually inspired Tom Jones? Why not Falstaff, the coward, or Oblomov, the sluggard, a man who, in a world of passion, discovered the delicacies of procrastination? Yes, Oblomov. Goncharov had it right, and after reading *Oblomov* we do not hate idleness, escapism, daydreaming; no, we love Oblomov.

I am hated for my ambition. I should have loved Oblomov more.

I have tried to be individualistic and have paid the price: friendlessness. I'm not complaining, it's the life I chose, a way of proceeding that owes nothing to any man. I don't pretend to have broken new ground like the men who throughout history took first steps down new roads. And the response to their efforts was often mockery and hatred. Consider some of the great inventions and the reactions to them. The automobile was considered foolish, the telephone a toy, the airplane impossible, the space ship a 25th-century fantasy. These were the results of creators working alone, men of vision, fighting, suffering, paying. But they were right, they won in the end, even though sometimes not in their lifetime.

I have no such illusions, but I wish to be cast in the same mould. No worthwhile work, I believe, is done collectively, by committee decision, but achieved under the guidance of a single individual thought. I am not a good team player.

One of my drinking companions once remarked that if I told him what a man finds sexually attractive, he would tell me that man's philosophy of life and his valuation of himself. I thought it drunken rambling at the time, but the more I think about it now, the more I believe it, even though I hate the conclusions I draw. He had pointed out that the man who has a good sense of his own value will want only a partner of quality, a challenge to him, someone to give him a sense of achievement; and that the other side of this, the observance of the mess that most men make of their sex lives, indicates a sense of worthlessness and a lack of any moral convictions.

I always thought that I aimed high, but in the end I followed what are — what must be — my deepest convictions, since I fully accepted my flaws, failings, character defects — call them what you will — as part of my make-up, thus damning myself to humility, and finding myself attracted to depravity, all that I seem to feel worthy of enjoying. Is it any wonder that shame was — is — my constant sexual companion?

How in hell did I get on to this? Never mind. Much as I hate to admit it, that evaluation is about right.

Should I destroy this story? I don't believe a legacy of disgrace is all I wish to leave behind — even if it's all there is.

Is it all there is? Is my life worth nothing more?

Destroy it? Yes, I think so, this territory is too dangerous to travel on paper. This and the rest of it must go. There is no point in putting on paper thoughts and the record of actions that may some day incriminate me. All of this should go into the furnace now, before we even get to the worst of it. Murder is such a merciless word, but I'm sure it will burn just as readily as any. So be it. Maybe I'll get around to burning it, maybe not. I'm always second-guessing myself.

CHAPTER 10

There were three reasons I decided to return home. One, I believed what I heard a Cape Bretoner say about Pictou, that when God was finished making the world he carelessly tossed all the bits and pieces left over into a garbage heap and called it Pictou. Two, there was a fight I wished to see coming up for the Maritime light-heavy championship, between Irish Leo Kelly and Bill Sparkes. Three, probably most important yet least defensible, I felt that my destiny, whatever it was to be, would be worked out at home on the Island.

I'd given up on my mother. In Halifax, I'd thought of her briefly, but didn't know where to begin looking. I studied the faces of women on the street, but couldn't even imagine what she'd look like now with the passage of years. By this time, anyway, my recollections of her were buried deep, surfacing rarely and then not for any length of time, and without the pangs that had ripped me in the beginning. Time passes; you bury your dead.

I knew that I would hear from Mae Costello's brothers, and I was home less than a week when I found them waiting for me one night as I left the New England Café. I had it coming so I didn't try to fight back, only to protect my head and privates. A vicious punch to my stomach brought up the Chinese food I'd gorged on and may have made them cut short the beating in disgust as I sprayed sweet and sour spare ribs and chicken chow mein indiscriminately. The two of them, Jacko and Tom, big men, cursed at me and nobbed me with their hard fists, and when I went down they put the boots to me, but I curled up and came out of the fray with a broken nose, two black eyes, assorted facial cuts and lumps, some bruised ribs, and black and blue marks all over my body.

It could have been worse, I guess — they could have killed me — although for the next couple of days that felt like it would have been a blessing.

Dr. Jack Sweeney, a friend and doctor to many West Enders, calmly smoked a cigarette as he poked, prodded, stitched, and bandaged. He was less than sympathetic. "Maybe this'll teach you to keep your pecker in your pants," he said with the faint trace of a grin. There are few secrets in a community like ours, which suited me fine this time. I wanted it known that I had taken my beating, paid for my sins. I paraded my battered body around town so that it would be seen that revenge had been meted out, honour satisfied. I wanted no strings attached to me. To my mind, a beating and a couple of weeks of discomfort were little enough to pay to escape from a marriage that would have been a disaster.

I attended the Kelly-Sparkes fight, like so many Islanders, wanting and expecting Kelly to win the title. He had beaten Cecil Braithwaite a few weeks earlier, and now, in our eyes, deserved the crown.

But Bill Sparkes was a wily, explosive fighter with dynamite in either fist. He and Leo battled on even terms through eight rounds, though it seemed that Leo was always playing catch-up, needing a rally every so often just to keep even with Sparkes who was pacing himself beautifully, always in control.

Then came the ninth round — and disaster. Sparkes straightened Leo up with a series of left jabs, then banged him with that punishing right hand. The crowd roared, the smoke hung around the lights, the air was thick with blood lust, and I felt that stomach-lurching that seized me when disaster was near. A boxing crowd wants a victim, even if it's one of their own. The thumbs-down of the Roman amphitheatre was never far removed from a boxing arena of the time. Sparkes feinted and threw his right — to the head, to the body, the head again, again the body — and Leo's eyes glazed. He stood in a corner, defenceless, while Sparkes pounded him, finally, mercifully, stepping back, looking in desperation at the referee, until big Joey MacDonald, seeing the passion die in the crowd, waved him away, wrapped his arms around the almost senseless Leo, and carried him to his corner.

I'd cringed as those hard fists pulverized poor Leo, feeling again the beating inflicted on me by Tom and Jacko Costello. The thought crossed my mind not for the first time that now that I'd done public penance for my sins I could entertain thoughts of payback — revenge for the revenge — but of the quiet kind, untraceable to me. I buried the thought quickly since this was not the time. Still, I remained aware that it would lie there, fermenting like home brew, and would surface and come to fruition in its own good time.

❖

I was back again at Mrs. Dunn's, hanging around the bowling alleys and the *Patriot* office, doing odd jobs, going out occasionally with the bootleggers' drivers to haul in a load of moonshine or corn whiskey, cashing cheques for the backroom poker players at any one of the five banks within a block of the alleys, bringing them food, picking up coffee and donuts at Reddin's or the Five-and-Ten for the *Patriot* workers, generally trying to make myself indispensable, although there was no real money in any of it. Never mind, I had made plenty during my stay in Pictou without having to deplete my stash, so these few dollars kept me in spending money for candy and cigarettes and the few drinks I was beginning to take at a quarter a shot, usually a couple of "shine sandwiches" — a shot of water, a shot of shine, a shot of water, the first water held in the mouth, diluting the strong liquor, allowing it to slip down the throat, the follow-up water buffeting it from the back end, preventing the burning, the inclination to heave, the danger of killing all sense of taste and rotting out the esophagus, the pleasant afterglow from even a couple or three shots creeping gradually through the body erasing tensions and inhibitions. Moonshine and corn whiskey came to be a panacea, a magic elixir, that, like the snake oil of the Wild West sideshow quacks, promised a cure for every ailment of the human spirit.

I took up again with Frankie Hanlan, not hanging around as obsequiously as before, but beginning to talk to him more as an equal, and with a friend of his, Everett Noonan. If Frankie was a dude, fussy about his clothing, no matter what he was wearing, always looking as if he'd had it cut specially for him, Ev Noonan always seemed ill-dressed, trying always by pulling and poking at his clothes to come to some accommodation with them, to the point where you felt like shouting at him to stop picking at himself, in the hope that everything would settle on him. Ev was skinny to the point of emaciation and appeared to care for nothing since he had nothing to hope for, a man very close to despair.

Still only twenty-nine, he'd spent five years in the Sanatorium on McGill Avenue with TB, a disease that at that time struck fear into people and claimed many each year on the Island. Ev had been thirty months in bed for twenty-four hours a day, up only when they made the bed around him and for a bed bath every second day.

Galloping TB is what Ev had, and if they hadn't used the needle to blow air into his lungs, he'd have been dead long ago. A hole was made in the bronchus, and when the air went in, the pus came up and out his mouth, as the air collapsed the lung, pushed up the poison. Rotten, rotten taste, but after five months that didn't work anymore, and the pus stayed in, and he had to lie still. "Remember your fibrosis," they'd say, those friendly, sympathetic nurses. "Don't raise your arms above your head." With the admonition to lie still, not even to move to use the bedpan or the urinal, he thought he'd go crazy. But he was sick most of the time, too sick to care, and he often wished for death, so that when he recovered, when he was back on the street and saw how difficult it was even to stay warm during an Island winter, he adopted a "try anything" attitude, determined to do what he could regardless of what it took, to better himself, and, conscious of his limited mortality, to enjoy the few years remaining to him.

He claimed belief in God, but wondered what God was doing all the time he'd been suffering, concluding that God was a handy fella to have around if thoughts of Him made you feel better, but that He really wasn't much good for doing anything to help. He bowed to inevitability; Everett Noonan became a true fatalist.

⁂

As I hung around the *Patriot* office, old Charlie Mitchell befriended me; the nuns' teaching solidified, and, since I appeared to have a liking for and a knack with words, he put up with me, letting me rewrite some of the brief stories of local baseball and hockey games by kids on the squares and ponds. Over time, I wrote scores of descriptions of games that took place at places like the Government Pond, the Jail Square, Victoria Park, and the river — any place, in fact, where a group of young males could get together to throw and bat a ball or skate and shoot a puck, to play and fight, and generally somehow squabble their way to a conclusion at the end of the day about who had won. Eager to see their names in the paper, one or two of the participants, usually one from each team so there would be no biased reporting, brought in the details: who drove in the winning run, who scored the goals, who made the big plays. I wrote it up, and I honestly believe that the brevity I learned then, how to cram the meat of a story into two or three paragraphs, was to remain with me throughout my newspaper days. It was all innocent enough, and old Charlie encouraged the kids, letting them know the paper was for them as well, making newspaper readers of them, if only the sports pages.

✹

It was an accepted fact that no one from the West End would be invited to join Rotary, the Gyros, the Kinsmen, or the Lions. The social strata did not descend into the West End, and even if invitations had been forthcoming, they would likely have been rejected since no one wished to be accused of putting on airs, of seeming to be better than his neighbours, of being stuck-up. "I remember you when the arse was out of your pants," was a common leveller, or "when the neighbours had to feed you," and this, of course, was the reason why the West End eventually changed and emptied: too many people wished to better themselves, wished for a better life, refusing to remain the hewers of wood and the drawers of water, refusing to remain in the lower stratum of society.

Oh, we had our prejudices, our pecking order. If the Irish were low on the totem pole, those of Acadian descent — the Frenchmen, as they were called — were lower still, even if the put-down was largely unconscious. It was never stated aloud, it was more subtle, an attitude, making fun of their accented talk — "singular, dis, dat; plural, dese, dose" — never mind that Irish intonations were often similar. We adopted a posture that said, in effect, we know we're low, but we do have you to look down on. And the blacks were down there, too, all three of us wallowing together in our inferiority, with an odd Scotsman thrown in to leaven the mix.

But there were plenty of good times, laughs, parties where the moonshine and home brew flowed — wakes and weddings, and, in this particular time, departures into the armed services. The young men joined mostly the army and navy; the air force was remarkably lacking in West End volunteers for no known reason. Even the Merchant Navy picked up a few who for medical reasons were rejected by the regular forces.

I was still too young at seventeen to join up myself, but I was big enough, so I tried anyway for the Navy. The doctors who examined me discovered an erratic heartbeat and turned me down. I went to the Army where, it was said, you'd be accepted as long as you could breathe. It so happened that was untrue. They, too, turned me down for the same reason.

We were living in modern times, or at least we thought we were, since that is the necessary illusion of every generation. We did not act as if we were preparing for some great post-war world. In our view, there was nothing quaint or colourful about us. We were ordinary people awash with the desire to survive, to arrive at old age, enjoying ourselves as much as possible along the way. We were not given much to soul-searching and introspection. My tricky heart meant nothing to me. I felt fine.

CHAPTER 11

1941 was ushered in with celebration. In *The Guardian* of January 2, the principal news items after the war headlines had to do with local New Year's activities. A class of some relative wealth, glittering in a setting of general mass misery, danced in the New Year at the Charlottetown Hotel (formerly the CN Hotel of fond memory), with a special floor show featuring a local group, "The Belles," under the direction of Mrs. (Dr.) J. P. Bell, with dinner at ten and dancing afterwards until two. Those entering the hotel for the feasting and festivities were greeted at the entrance by a horde of drunks celebrating in their own loutish way, and who hurled a barrage of insults, some of them quite funny, at the couples as they exited their vehicles and climbed the five steps to the front door to be greeted by young Matt Malone and Lorne Casford, both destined shortly for the armed services, but already displaying the ease with people that was to be the hallmark of their long careers at the hotel after the war.

There was a dance as well at the Legion on Grafton Street, a skate at the Forum, a special midnight movie at the Prince Edward. Both City Police and the RCMP reported guilelessly that "everything was quiet and orderly and law-abiding."

Neither Frankie Hanlan nor Ev Noonan nor myself attended any of these parties, ha, ha. We brought in the New Year in our own way with a couple of bottles of corn whiskey in our rooms at Mrs. Dunn's. Ev lived at home, but he may as well have been a roomer with us since he spent many nights on a tick rolled into a corner of Frankie's room.

Much of our talk centred on ways to make money — a few quick dollars. Well, more than a few, a great many.

"We could stick up a bank," Ev said, the alcohol doing wonders for his complexion — and his mind.

"You're joking," Frankie said.

"I know it."

"Hold on a minute," I said. "Not a bank, but what about a store?"

"Who?"

"How do I know. Who's got money?"

"Nobody we know," said Ev.

We drank on it for a while. After a bit, I said, "There's got to be someone around here who's doing okay."

"Nawww," Ev said.

"Maybe a drugstore," Frankie said. "Vic Coyle's?"

"Too close to the police station," I said.

"A jewellery store," Ev suggested. "Ches Campbell's?"

"What'd we do with a bunch of jewellery?" I asked.

"Sell it."

"Sure, and be in jail the next day."

"You know," Ev said, "for a kid you've got a lot to say."

"Glad you noticed, Ev. It's one of my best points."

Corn whiskey has its uses. They both laughed; good humour prevailed.

"No, but some storekeeper or other," I said. "Frankie?"

He was in and out of stores with goods from the wholesalers every day.

"I don't know. Some pay in cash, others by cheque. There's not too many—" He broke off.

"What?"

"I was just thinking — Peter Hogan."

Bingo!

"He always pays cash," Frankie said. "And you often hear that he got a stash."

"Yeah," Ev said. "I heard that."

"Well, then," I said.

It was as simple as that. I must have a mean streak in me. I was young, I had possibilities, I had no worries about ready cash for a time, but after being turned down by Peter Hogan for a job, although the rejection was handled courteously, I wanted to strike out at the old man in some way, to teach him that he should have listened to the request of a reasonable person since now, by God, we'd take it all.

"No violence," Ev said. "We got no call to hurt the old man."

"No violence," Frankie agreed. "We won't need to."

I nodded my assent. "When?"

"Later in the month," Frankie said.

"When it ain't so goddam cold," Ev said.

We all laughed and had another drink.

✳

It was a time of good news for me when I heard in mid-January of Mae Costello's miscarriage. It had happened late in her pregnancy, and the word was that she'd had a hard time of it and barely pulled through herself. I felt a pang of remorse and a moment of sorrow for Mae, but it did not extend to making me want to do anything about it. Anyway, I told myself as I hardened my heart, it was as much her fault as mine.

There was no possibility of a reunion with Mae, but the thought of money claims on me by our child of the sun was a spectre that had flitted through my mind from time to time. Now I was completely free of her, and I began to think dark thoughts about her brothers. This was an omen, I told myself, and I took it almost as a command to invest some time considering ways to inflict punishment on them.

I hate it when it's too simple. One likes a challenge. With Jacko and Tom Costello, it was almost with a sense of regret that I took time away from other things to deal with them, but I made it up to myself when, after first deciding to seek them out separately, I changed my mind and decided to increase the risk, raise the ante, by taking them both on at the same time.

Disguise was important — I didn't want them coming at me again — so I bought a fold-back toque and cut a couple of eyeholes in it, making it into a balaclava. My clothes were dark anyway, my boots heavy, and, to make the odds more even, I armed myself with a three-foot length of steel bar. Each of them had at least twenty-five pounds on me, so to my way of thinking we now had the makings of a fair fight.

One night amid brief snow flurries, I followed them from their home to a bootlegger's down east on Richmond Street. I hoped they'd be settled in for at least a couple of hours, so I hid the bar under the snow and went uptown to the Roxy for a sandwich and a couple of cups of coffee. About eleven, I said to the waitress, "What're you doing later tonight, Doreen?" and set up a date with her for after work. Maria Thomas, daughter of the owner, a pretty girl a few years older, made a slapping motion in my direction, grinning.

"You'd be bad news for a girl, Mickey."

"Maria, how could you? I'm saving myself for you."

She laughed, the hearty laugh of a comfortable woman. "That'll be the day." Maria had a steady boyfriend, Buck Mc-Carville, who ran the nearby taxi stand.

Back at the bootlegger's, I dug up the bar, hiding myself in the inner shadows of the gangway. I had to wait almost an hour, which was okay with me since they'd be worse off for drink.

Traffic was now all one way — leaving. Each time someone left I pulled down my mask and hefted the bar, but none of the leavers were the Costellos. I had just about decided they must have slipped away earlier when Harry, the bootlegger, opened the door, calling, "Okay," then, "See you later, boys," and they stepped into the gangway. Harry closed the door, and I could hear the two-by-four being slammed into its steel brackets, then the light over the door went out.

I let them take a few steps then came up quickly behind them, calling softly, hoarsely, deepening my voice, "Hey, Jacko." They stopped and turned. Jacko was the one nearest me, and I rammed the end of the steel pipe like a bayonet into his gut, and he gasped, his mouth open like a landed fish, then he toppled over. The drink slowed Tom, but he was quick for all that and aimed a boot at me that I caught in mid-air with the bar as I came onto him with a baseball swing that DiMaggio would have envied, feeling the leg shatter, hearing his shriek as he went down. Moving fast, I swung back with the bar to Jacko and broke his arm. I booted both of them in the face, feeling bone and gristle give, and then I was out of the gangway, hurrying, just as Harry's light came on again, the whole evolution taking less than ten seconds.

I ran, excitement filling me, a sense of accomplishment at a job well done. I hid the bar under the snow by the Court House, met Doreen, and was home in bed within the hour. I rediscovered the joy, the elation, of violence, the energy it gave me, the sense of impending explosion. Guilt was something that did not even enter my consciousness. I slept little that night.

I had not called Emily Kate since I'd come home, but the next day, still exuberant, I did so.

"I came back last week," I said, smiling. You can always tell a smile on the phone.

"Hooray," she said. "Don't you mean three weeks ago?"

"Oh."

"'Oh' indeed. Thanks for remembering me."

"Yeah, well, I've—"

"I know. You've been busy."

"Look, Emily Kate, I just wanted to let you know I'm back. Does it really matter how long?"

"I guess not. Well, thanks for calling."

"Wait a minute," I said. "Who told you?"

"Does it really matter who told me?" she said snidely. "But for your information it was Billy."

"Billy Williams?"

"Yes, of course."

"Okay," I said. "I'll see you soon."

"Sure," she said.

The phone banged in my ear.

More problems, I thought. What was Billy Williams up to, keeping track of me? Or was it just one of those things where he had seen me and mentioned it in talking to Emily Kate? Don't get paranoid, I told myself, it's just a coincidence.

CHAPTER 12

I'd like you to know something of the times, the places, the people. Yeats wrote that the history of a people is not in parliaments, but in what people say to each other on fair-days and high days, and how they farm and quarrel. While fair-days and farming were pretty light on the ground in the West End, people talked and fought and the rest of it, and you could get a pretty good idea of how we lived if you hung out there for a few days.

It was a neighborhood thing, the customs of where you lived. If I had lived out near the Exhibition Grounds, I would have caddied and played golf at Belvedere; if I'd lived in the East End, I'd have played ball and hockey on the mussel mud and felt the domination of the CNR since all around me would be railway families; if I'd lived in Brighton, I'd have played tennis in Victoria Park and attended the Saturday afternoon teas and generally been unaware of people like me. We were like fingerprints — the same but different.

If, as had happened, Jack Dempsey came to town, the fact that he spoke at a fundraiser, that he was interviewed by Loman McAulay over CFCY, "The Friendly Voice of the Maritimes," played no part in our thinking. What was important was that one day out walking, he had wandered into the West End and spent an hour talking about his early hard times with us kids and some old-timers on a bench on the Jail Square. That visit — and his re-enactment of the famous "Long Count" — that was ours, and it didn't matter what Jack Dempsey's real purpose was in coming to Charlottetown, that satisfied our idea of fame, that marked us as a spot in the world, ensured that we were known, that our vistas were similar to those of the great, and by this association the world at large was made aware of our neighborhood, our end of town. It was our way of saying we were somebody.

In the homes I knew about there was a certain similarity to the entertainment, with cards and radio shows predominating: rummy, cribbage, 45s, and shows like "Gang Busters," "The Kraft Music Hall" with Bing Crosby, "The Chase and Sanborn Hour" with Edgar Bergen and Charlie McCarthy, "The Green Hornet," "Jack Benny," "Fibber McGee and Molly," "The Lone Ranger." The radios themselves in stores like Toombs and Miller Brothers carried names out of radio history: Marconi, Philco, Stromberg-Carlson. In my boarding house on late fall Saturday afternoons, I would crouch before the old RCA Victor table model, straining to hear the frenetic announcer on the short wave from South Bend, Indiana, over the static, the fading signal, and, always, the faint Morse code in the background, relaying the excitement of the fighting Irish of Notre Dame toiling against the Boilermakers of Purdue, the Illini, or the Trojans of Southern California. Huddling against the radio, a nickel's worth of chewy candy from The Sugar Bowl clutched in my feverish fists, I zigzagged up and down the field, mentally struggling with the concepts of a game I knew little about, gradually coming to understand it well enough to enjoy the feats of my Saturday afternoon heroes, those in the land of radio but who lived in the real world and who were more — or less — than fellows like Flash Gordon, Tim Tyler, or Buck Jones, whose existence depended on "the funnies" or the brightness of the movie screen.

❋

The three of us, Frankie Hanlan, Ev Noonan, and myself, were products of a Catholic autocracy, of Irish guilt and wish to please, of obeisance before the idea of eternity, hounded by religious confusion; yet, at the same time, defiant, and, in the concentration camp atmosphere of Queen Square School, familiar with the free use of the fist and strap. And when we saw Skippy Hayes beaten so badly that he crawled under his desk sobbing, wetting his pants, the lessons of brutality were not lost on us. Brutality brought fear — and obedience.

I cannot speak for the others, but even as I cried "*Non serviam*" in moments of doubt and insecurity, religious questions weighed heavily on me, such as, What if the priests and nuns are right? What if our every move is recorded for or against us? What if there is a hell? And I pondered why I considered my thinking superior, more profound than so many Fathers of the Church; and I would look into myself and find myself wanting, and hasten into an Act of Contrition and vow to do better, all of which would disappear into the limbo where good intentions die at the first return of self-confidence. I had depended on myself for too long, and, while it hadn't all been roses, I had endured, I had survived. I found it hard — impossible — to submit, and to strengthen my resolve and confidence I repeated to myself, although not in these words, my belief that there is no absurdity so palpable but that it may be firmly planted in the human mind if only you begin to inculcate it early in a child's life by constantly repeating it with an air of great authority. In this regard, the Catholic Church had done its job well. My attention waned at Sunday Mass until I gradually slipped into the lukewarm category, my attendance falling off except when my guilt became too great, and I would crawl back seeking forgiveness.

Some of my most religious moments I encountered while drinking in Billy LeBlanc's, like the time we were singing there, myself, Frankie, and Ev, harmonizing mournfully, joyously, and profoundly out of the depths of our Irish-Catholic-Queen-Square-School souls.

In her eyes there's the light of Killarney
In her cheeks there's the rose of Kildare,

In her voice just a wee bit of Blarney,
And the snow of Athlone in her hair...

We drove everybody out of the bootlegger's except Billy himself; even Bill's brother Lal, whose Acadian soul craved a bit of song and dance, left, muttering to himself about the "friggin' Irishmen." Some might say it was only sentiment, but I shall always believe that in my hardening soul such moments were as close as I was capable of coming to religious experiences.

✳

About this time, too, I discovered that Emily Kate was working in Charlottetown as a clerk in Ray's Confectionery next to the Prince Edward Theatre. For a while I watched her, noting the fine good looks of her, the long red hair, the shapely swing of her walk, even from a distance the flashing eyes. From a gangly youngster she had grown into a beautiful young woman. The crowd who hung around Ray's were mostly from West Kent School and Brighton, and I knew what they'd be like, sniffing around Emily Kate, so I decided to stop in and see her.

I bought a chocolate bar and said, "Remember me?"

She looked at me without smiling. "Who could forget?"

I looked around, embarrassed. "I'd like to have a talk with you, Emily Kate." I sounded stilted, awkward, even to myself.

"Why? Your phone out of order?"

I let that pass.

"To get caught up. To discuss...this." My hand, my glance encompassed the store.

She smiled without mirth. "You don't like where I work?"

"No, no. I just thought...we could talk...."

Another customer was impatiently tapping a coin against the glass case.

"I have to go."

"Yes, well, can I see you?"

She hesitated briefly. "Tonight. Eight o'clock." She mentioned an address on Weymouth Street, then turned away.

When I called, she was still in her work clothes, including the neat white apron.

"We're not going anywhere," she said in answer to my raised eyebrows.

"But I thought we could—"

"You said talk. We can talk here."

"Uh — okay."

"So — talk. Tell me what you've been doing."

I told her — briefly, emphasizing the few months I'd worked in Pictou, making it sound like a year or longer. I talked about the job at Fisher Brothers, but skipped quickly to my work at the newspaper, modestly telling her of the good things Charlie Mitchell had said about my writing, voicing my gratitude to her for making me read so much back in our orphanage days. My deflections and misdirections didn't work with Emily Kate.

"Fisher Brothers. Isn't that where you met Mae Costello?"

"I took her out a few times."

"They say you got her pregnant."

"Well 'they' got it wrong. She didn't have a baby."

"They say you made her get an abortion."

To hell with it, it was no secret, and God knows I had worn my humiliation publicly enough after her brothers beat the crap out of me.

"It was a miscarriage."

"So you did get her pregnant?"

"Look, Emily Kate, are you proposing to give me absolution — or what?"

"And I suppose you know nothing about what people are calling the revenge beating of her brothers?"

"So help me God, Emily Kate, I know absolutely nothing about that. Even the police cleared me on that one."

"Did you know one of them has a punctured lung?"

"No, I hadn't heard." That at least was true. My surprise was genuine. The iron bar, I thought, that'd do it. "But it serves the son-of-a-bitch right."

"The other brother may be coming after you again."

"If he comes near me again I'll kill him."

She nodded. "As wise as ever, aren't you?"

"Dammit, Emily Kate. I don't want to talk about her or her bastard brothers."

"And as genteel."

"And how's yourself, Emily Kate?"

"What happened to your cousin?"

"Old Doyle? Heart attack."

"Things seem to happen to people around you."

"It was a heart attack, Emily Kate.... But enough about me. I want to talk about you."

She softened enough to tell me about her life since the orphanage: being adopted, feeling secure, then the fondling, the fear, the running away, the return to the orphanage, her work there in the school until she felt confident enough to move out on her own.

I sat there, nodding, letting her talk, not breaking her concentration, a trick to encourage candidness that she herself had taught me many years ago.

"You've no idea how it feels," she said.

"They shoulda beat the crap out of the guy," I said.

"Brilliant," she sniffed.

She briefly considered the sisterhood as a vocation, seeing its safety and its power, but decided she was too worldly for the call to God.

"What about Mary Magdalene?" I asked after she fell silent.

"I'm not a whore."

"I just meant—"

"I know what you meant."

We were sitting in the parlour. It was quiet as if we were alone, but the elderly couple she roomed with, James and Hazel MacDonald, were out back in the kitchen, so we kept our voices down.

"That crowd—" I began.

"Who?"

"Around Ray's. They'll be after you."

"So that's what this's about. You're playing big brother."

"Not at all," I protested. "I just think you should know—"

"I know about boys — and the boys around Ray's are real gentlemen — compared to some."

Subtlety was not Emily Kate's strong point. I nodded but said nothing, knowing there was no way I could win.

"And I see Billy now and again."

Jealousy stabbed me. Eventually, I said, "I better go."

"It was...good to see you," she said.

"And you, Emily Kate.... Can I see you again?"

"I don't know. Why?"

"We could go to a show maybe...?"

"Oh, I don't know. When?"

"Say...next Monday night?"

"Well...okay...I guess...."

Her enthusiasm was less than overwhelming. I touched the back of her hand with one finger, said "Good night," and left.

Do I want to get into this? I asked myself on the way home. Where will it lead? Am I serious about Emily Kate, or is it my desire to see her safe, or simply that in my selfishness

I don't want anyone else to have her? Can I give a girl any-thing? And even as these questions were troubling me, a part of my black brain was calculating, as it had so many years ago, how I could use Emily Kate to my own best advantage, and way back in the recesses of my resentful mind an on-and-off neon flickered, reminding me that not once had the damned redhead called me by name.

✳

At the paper I got my first break on a story when Pete Carragher came down sick, and I was assigned to cover a hockey game at the Forum. A fight broke out on the ice, and when referee Willie Larkin gave RCAF player Roy Bendrick a major, words ensued and on the way to the penalty box, Bendrick drew off and belted Larkin. But Willie Larkin was no man to trifle with; he bounced up and grabbed the larger Bendrick by the front of his sweater and hit him once with a right hand, breaking his jaw and thereby ending the discus-sion.

In those days, referees were permitted — expected even — at least at the local level — to defend themselves, to protect their own interests. The fans cheered Larkin who had been a popular player in his day, then a coach, and was now a re-spected referee.

I was off and running. My lead paragraph set the tone for the story: "Roy Bendrick's wired-up jaw will cause him hun-ger pangs over the next few weeks, after he learned last night to his chagrin that there are darn few vitamins to be gained from chewing on the hide of referee Willie Larkin."

It wasn't great, but it is still my personal favourite from the hundreds of leads I was to write over the years. When I showed it to Emily Kate, she was suitably impressed and gave me that all-teeth-and-freckles-smile that made my heart leap.

In my mind, I was right up there with "The Front Page"

bunch, a member of the newspaper breed: young, full of beans, with a dislike of routine and order, and a love of the new, the ever-changing challenge.

Old Charlie Mitchell had been right that day he showed me around the *Patriot* pressroom: it gets in your blood. I considered myself a reporter, already equipped with the newspaperman's waspish belief that the public has room in its brain for only one story at a time. I was sure more than ever that my Grade Ten education and my wide reading were enough learning for anyone.

In many ways I was a product of my times and environment: street smart, with a cynic's view of the goodness of my fellow man. In other ways, particularly in the politics of any situation, I knew so little, I was so naive. But that realization came only later.

CHAPTER 13

There was a record snowfall in January 1941, more than 54 inches, topped off towards the end of the month with nine more inches that threw the province into confusion. The Borden train, which usually arrived at 8 P.M., crept into Charlottetown after 1 A.M., and the *Abegweit*, because of the storm and heavy drift ice, was taking more than four hours to make the usual one-hour crossing. When the roads became impassable, many airmen from the base on Brackley Point Road and soldiers from Beach Grove Inn found to their delight that they had to find lodgings in the city at hotels or in the homes of accommodating friends. Sailors stationed at HMCS Queen Charlotte on Kent Street had no such excuse, but many went AWOL anyway in hopes of forgiveness from Regulating CPO Stan Bowles.

Bootleggers thrived.

The next day was for digging out, the temperature in the late afternoon dropping well below freezing, the winds picking up to gale force with further snow flurries adding to the general misfortune.

Out in Brighton, Mrs. Ross, wife of merchant prince Chester R. Ross, drew the chintz living room drapes, let the cat in, advanced the dial on the new kitchen oil stove a couple of degrees, called down to the handyman in the basement to stoke up the furnace with the best Old Sydney Screened coal, placed two well-seasoned birch logs carefully on the fireplace in the well-appointed den, and, with a sense of accomplishment, after battening down the hatches, carried herself with dignity upstairs to dress for dinner and await the arrival of himself.

In the West End, Mrs. Gormley, wife of labourer Peter Gormley, prayed that the banking would hold and keep out the worst of the cold, prepared the thunder mugs so that none of the children would have to go out to the freezing outhouse, and hoped that young Tommy would be home soon from his forage to Weeks's Coal Yard out in Irishtown with enough stolen coal to see them through another night.

It was ideal weather for a crime.

✳

The plan was simple. I was to keep a lookout, then around midnight Frankie and Ev and I'd go in, hoping that old Hogan would be asleep, but if not we'd just knock him on the head and clean him out.

I huddled in the corner by Packy Morrison's, kitty-corner from the store, and saw Bill Ryness amble down King Street — even in the cold Bill ambled. He entered the store, stayed about ten minutes, and left. After some time the lights went out. As my watch crept towards midnight, I crossed to the front door and listened but heard nothing. To warm myself up, I walked up the street to Angus MacEachern's garage, then back down towards the wharf, then around the block and back to my lookout position. Frankie and Ev came along about midnight from the late movie at the Capitol, and, by the smell of them, from a bootlegger's as well.

"Everything okay?" Frankie asked.

"The lights are out. It's quiet."

We crossed the street, our feet squeaking in the snow. At the door, Frankie pulled a narrow metal strip, like a ruler, from an inside pocket. There was no deadbolt, and we were inside within a minute, locking the door behind us. The familiar smell that I remembered from Doyle's store filled the air, mingled with the rich aroma from the cookie bins.

The floor creaked beneath our weight. We quieted down, listening, hearing a sound like a person turning over in bed. Frankie had his hand on my arm, settling me. It was dark, but the glow of the streetlight on the corner threw a patch of light into a corner of the store.

"Follow me," Frankie whispered, and we crept across to the door leading to the rear. The door opened slowly, silently, as Frankie nudged it, and we glided stealthily into the darkened room, leaving the door ajar to admit a little light. We were picking our way through this storeroom, Frankie in front, Ev off to one side, me in the rear, when Frankie went, "Look out!" and a gun cracked.

"Christ!" Ev shouted and jumped aside.

Old Hogan was astride Frankie on the floor, choking him. I felt around for something, anything, to hit him with. Frankie was gasping and grunting, losing the battle. Ev cringed against the wall, hopeless, the peacemaker who'd insisted on no violence.

My hand swept over a table, found a knife. I jabbed it into the back of Hogan's neck, hauling it across, dragging him by the hair off Frankie, who jumped to his feet, grabbed the knife from me and began punching and slashing indiscriminately with it.

Blood spurted. Hogan's body sagged like a sack of flour to the floor.

"Are you hit?" I asked Frankie.

"No — went by my face...the old bastard," he said, giving the still body a kick.

I wiped the knife off on the body and slipped it into my jacket pocket.

"Jesus," Frankie said, rubbing his neck. "He's a strong old bastard — near choked me."

"Is he dead?" Ev hadn't moved from the wall. "The blood shot all over me." He was rubbing at his coat.

"Just wounded," Frankie said, pocketing the gun. "Let's go."

We put on a light in the back room, started to tear it apart looking for the stash. We found nothing. A pool of blood formed on the floor beside the body.

I nodded towards the body. "Don't you think we better call...."

"Never mind him," Frankie said. "Out front."

We went back into the store, pulled the blinds, turned on the light, rang open the cash register. Nothing.

"The old son-of-a-bitch," Frankie shouted, banging the cash register with his fist. We rifled the shelves, pocketing cigarettes and bars, shoving things aside, searching. Nothing. We paused and lit up smokes.

There was a rattle at the door.

"Open up. Police."

"Holy Jesus," Ev gasped. "What'll we do?"

"Upstairs," Frankie shouted, tugging at his pocket as the glass broke in the door. He aimed the pistol and pulled the trigger but the gun had jammed, probably why old Hogan hadn't finished him off. Frankie dropped the gun on the steps as we fled. We were in a narrow hallway, a window into the backyard at one end.

"Out the window," Ev shouted, breaking it out with a chair.

"To hell with that," Frankie said. "They'll have it covered."

"I'm going," Ev said, hanging from his fingers, dropping into the snow below.

I glanced out the window in time to see a policeman grab the helpless Ev, wedged up to his thighs in the deep snow, struggling to haul himself loose. Handcuffs flashed in the moonlight.

"They got him," I said softly, but Frankie paid no attention, his gaze fixed on the head of the stairs.

"Come on up," he called to the police below.

Footsteps started up. There was a case of Seaman's pop along the wall — the large bottles — and Frankie hefted one of these by the neck. As the policeman's head rose above the stairwell, Frankie swung a smashing blow, and he tumbled back down the stairs.

There was more noise as reinforcements rushed in the front door. I took a quick look out the broken window. Nobody. I hoisted myself up, preparing to drop. "Come on, Frankie. There's no one back here now."

He took a quick look over his shoulder at me, but the idea of flight was foreign to his self-image. He shook his head, muttered, "Go, go," then turned back to the stairs, shouting in the best gangster tradition, "Come and get me."

I let go and dropped into the snow, burrowing out and away to the echo of crashing and banging from the top floor of Peter Hogan's store. I was home and in the warmth of my bed in fifteen minutes, trembling, lying awake throughout the night, waiting for the police to come for me, the knife buried in a snowbank behind the house.

All the next day I functioned in a world of unreality. The morning *Guardian* had the glaring front-page headline: "Aged Charlottetown Resident Killed in Store," with two sub-heads reading: "Body of Peter Hogan Found in Pool of Blood," and "Two Men Taken into Custody by Police Early Today; Evidence of Struggle."

I am really for it this time, I thought, flight never far from my mind. The coroner ordered an inquest, and a jury was struck. Details at this point were scarce, but there was no mention anywhere of a third person.

The Guardian the next day, Saturday, carried an editorial which began, "The brutal crime reported in yesterday's *Guardian*...has caused province-wide indignation and alarm...." and an inside page contained all known details and photos of Hogan, his store front, the broken upstairs window, and the blood stains in the storeroom. There was no mention of a third person, nor of the murder weapon. The story said simply: "One of Mr. Hogan's meat knives, or a similar knife, is assumed to have been the murder weapon."

Officers Wellman and Lank were the officers on foot patrol along Pownal Street who saw the light come on in the store behind the drawn blind, checked it, and heard the shouted, "The old son-of-a-bitch." Lank went next door to phone for backup and when they saw the patrol rounding the corner from Richmond Street, they began banging on the door.

Officers Powell and Gregg had been in the paddy wagon near Fred Lambros's corner when they got the message on the recently installed two-way radio, and sped to the scene in time for Powell to be the arresting officer as Ev Noonan came tumbling out the rear window, and for Gregg to be the one clobbered with the pop bottle as he ran up the stairs.

In reply to the "Come and get me" challenge, Wellman and Lank charged up the stairs, a thrown chair and an iron bar glancing off them before they wrestled Frankie to the floor.

It is fair to say that for days, perhaps weeks, I functioned in a state of paralysis waiting for the other shoe to drop. It was beyond my comprehension that these two, particularly the weaker Noonan, would be willing to accept responsibility for the act — I had trouble saying murder — the craven snivelling of the criminal caught in the act requiring him to point elsewhere, anywhere, in his compulsion to free himself from blame. But no, they didn't implicate me, and I dared to hope, realizing that the longer they waited, the less likely anyone would be to believe them.

The inquest revealed that the body had suffered the indignity of twenty-two knife wounds, but that "the wound in the back of the neck positively caused the death," according to Dr. D. J. McGuire who had performed the autopsy. "The head," he said, "was about two-thirds severed from the body by a knife similar to Mr. Hogan's meat knives, and honed to razor sharpness."

My heart sank. This was confirmation that the rip I'd given with the knife across the back of Hogan's neck had been the death blow. Did Hanlan know that, I wondered. Not likely. I concluded that he would think that the way he savaged Hogan's body had incidentally included the neck wound. It was no consolation to know I was again a murderer, but still I hoped for Hanlan's continued silence.

On one of those early days there appeared in *The Guardian* a picture of Frankie and Ev being led from the Police Station to the patrol for a trip to the Court House. About thirty people are crowded around, all male, all in caps or hats, all in profile or seen from the rear, except one in the immediate foreground, full face, an earlug cap pulled down, eyes staring at the camera, a picture of myself reflecting — what? It could have been a sense of wonder, but I knew it was fear. In that photo, I saw my own guilt, and I waited with mounting expectation for someone else to detect the obvious.

The community was outraged and talked of little else. "I knew that pair'd come to no good end," was heard often from those who knew everything. Because of the circumstances, the blood on their clothing, the stolen goods in their pockets, the police testimony that "there was nobody else in the house but Hanlan, Noonan, and the dead man," there was no doubt in anyone's mind that they were guilty.

A brief announcement appeared on a back page in *The Guardian* to the effect that "the City Police will in future be armed," sparking a savage anti-guns-for-police editorial which told how for scores of years Islanders were reputed to be the most law-abiding and exemplary people in the wide Dominion, that serious crime was practically unknown here, that many citizens go to bed at night without even bothering to lock their doors.

Despite this editorial, *The Guardian* carried a story a couple of days later that "four shiny new revolvers destined for use by the City Police were placed on display at Fennell and Chandler's Hardware Store yesterday. It is understood that two of these will be supplied to police on night duty immediately, and it is expected more will follow later. The revolvers are .38 calibre centre-firing with safety hammer and double action."

And on the same page, a simple notice appeared stating that Peter Hogan's funeral had been held yesterday with Mass at St. Dunstan's Basilica and burial in the church cemetery.

I followed every item of news in both papers — *The Guardian*, since it was a morning paper, usually breaking the news of the night before, the evening *Patriot* offering slightly different versions of the same stories, and, for variety, often going after the unusual angle or doing feature stories, and, of course, breaking any stories that came its way. Basically, however, both were of the opinion that this was pretty much an open-and-shut case.

One night in March as the ice in the harbour was breaking up, I retrieved the knife from behind the house, took it under my jacket down to the Railway Wharf, and heaved it as far as I could into the waves.

✳

The trial was scheduled for June, and gradually I began to feel less fearful, counting more and more on Frankie's arrogance, his desire for notoriety, his contradictory statements of innocence, and the oft-reported threat he'd made to the police that if he'd been able to get the pistol working they'd never have taken him. What never ceased to amaze me was how he managed to get Ev Noonan to go along and not involve me, but as I thought more about it, as I pondered their claim to innocence, I came to realize that they could not now bring me into it without damage to their own case.

My friend Leo O'Connell was representing Hanlan and Noonan, opposite Attorney-General Thomas Caldwell, assisted by Charles Tracey.

Other news intervened during the weeks awaiting the trial: "Tobruk Battle Still Raging"; "Cruiser 'Hood' Sunk by Enemy Action"; "Conn Flails Louis For 12 Rounds Before Being Subdued in 13th."

✻

The trial was played out as if the conclusion were foreordained. The evidence was straightforward, and witnesses, the principal ones being the police, were led through their paces unerringly by Mr. Caldwell or Mr. Tracey. Poor Leo O'Connell had little to go on, little to question, so he repeatedly reminded all concerned that all the evidence was circumstantial, that no one had seen the murder committed, that the murder weapon was never recovered, even though the two men were apprehended at the scene, that they could just as easily have come along after the deed, that they could have bloodstains on their clothing from tripping over the body, and that nothing had been proved "beyond a reasonable doubt." As well, a "third man" theory developed, the story of a third man being seen around the store close to midnight, and Leo threw that into the mix to sow seeds of doubt, to make it as difficult for the jury as possible — "perhaps this third man took away the missing weapon." Little did he know how close to the truth he was!

The Crown concluded strongly by calling the police officers who had been on the scene. The case was nailed down as tight as a coffin lid.

Opening for the defence, Leo O'Connell said that some remarkable statements had been made but not proved, and that he would call several witnesses to clear his clients, and that they themselves would testify although he had advised them not to since, in the absence of the weapon, "which proves the presence of a third man," he did not think it necessary. They wished, however, "to put an end to the gossip and slander going on against them for the past six months."

He dwelt on the third-man scenario, bringing forth a witness to the fact that indeed the third man existed. Benjamin Gallant, who lived across the street, said he'd seen a man at the door close to midnight, but that he didn't know if he was just leaving or trying to get into the store, that the man went north a bit then turned back south towards the waterfront and out of sight. My perambulations to stay warm had been witnessed!

Hanlan and Noonan should have heeded their lawyer's advice not to testify since they did themselves no good. Hanlan said that they saw a light in the store and decided to get some pop or two-percent beer, but that they had no knowledge of Mr. Hogan's death until they were accused. From the far corner, they saw the lights go out and a man leave. They didn't know him. They went in and "sang out," but there was no answer, so they went into the back room where, in the darkness, they both tripped over what they took to be a bag of flour. Then they went back out front and began to work the cash register, hoping the noise would bring Mr. Hogan into the store. They then heard the police at the front door, and ran upstairs. Hanlan said, "I was afraid of being arrested as it would damage my social standing." He was just "an ordinary fellow," he said, and the police would not arrest "the big shots" under the same circumstances.

Noonan claimed he'd done nothing wrong, "but the cops just don't seem to believe me." The third man had come out of the store "at a fast walk" before they crossed over and entered. They saw nothing but "a big darkness" in the storeroom. When they ran upstairs, he wasn't trying to escape out the window, but tripped, and his momentum carried him out, glass and all. When Chief Birtwhistle read him the charge of murder the next day, "I thought he was just trying to sober me up."

The Crown didn't push hard on cross-examination, wishing to avoid overkill.

In summary, O'Connell claimed it was all circumstantial, and that the police were remiss in not bringing to justice the real murderer, the third man, who, in all likelihood, carried the murder weapon away with him. This man was seen by the two accused and by witness Benjamin Gallant. He said the case against the two men had not been proved beyond all reasonable doubt, and the jury should acquit. He asked the jury how they would feel if they found the defendants guilty and later this third man, the real murderer, turned up.

Attorney-General Caldwell coasted with the evidence: the blood-stained clothing, the stolen goods found on the men, their earlier statements, the recollection of events by the police. The mystery man, he said, was obviously someone who'd tried the door, found it locked, and left. The missing knife, he said, could have been disposed of on the way back to the police station.

"It would have been easy," Caldwell said, "to flip the knife into a snowbank along the way, and for it to be raked up with all the dirt and refuse in the spring." He begged the jury not to allow sympathy to prejudice them.

In addressing the jury, Judge J. A. Smithers said that, instead of just dealing with the essential features of the case, he intended to go into every detail of evidence "as exhaustively as lies within my power and ability."

He said, "I shall give you the benefit of my ideas as to how this crime was committed from the evidence submitted in the case...but remember they are only my ideas."

In a lengthy harangue that would never pass today as in any way objective or disinterested, including leaving the Bench to act out his version of events, Judge Smithers then as much as made the case again for the Crown, leaving no doubt of his position, while assuring the jury several times that "you are the sole judge of the facts," and "it is your privilege to disregard all I may say. But personally," he added, "I cannot see how any man could possibly have any reasonable doubt as to who committed this crime."

After being thus browbeaten, is it any wonder that after six days of trial, during which twenty-seven witnesses were heard, the "twelve men and true" took only a half-hour to find Hanlan and Noonan guilty of murder? A few days later the judge, possibly regretting the passing of the "hanged, drawn, and quartered" of a bygone era, meted out the punishment: hanging, to be carried out on 20 August.

Back in February the same judge had given Jerry Dupuis twenty-five years for manslaughter in the killing of a relative, and the wits observed that this time he was merely looking to correct his oversight.

The prisoners took the verdict without any outward emotion, Hanlan showing a spark of grace and dignity, probably in keeping with his self-image, when he thanked all concerned, especially Leo O'Connell, while reiterating their innocence. Judge Smithers urged the men to make a full confession in writing, "to demonstrate to those who may follow in your footsteps" that crime does not pay.

Poor Frankie. He so wanted the press and radio to install him in the same hierarchy they reserved for royalty, athletic heroes, movie stars, and big-time crooks. Instead, they reported what he said without lustre or embellishment, without allowing him to define himself through his fantasies, leaving him in the end a bewildered, pathetic figure.

Is it possible that in his megalomania he was unaware of how profoundly he had failed to create the image he wished to present to the people of the Island? Is it possible that the desire for recognition combined with cold amorality could so blind him that in the end as he stood there condemned to die he could have no realization of how empty it all was?

Yes, probably. Frankie's response to the death penalty: "We all have to die. What's a few years more or less?" He was twenty-five years old at the time.

The Guardian of 20 August carried the story: "Executions this morning at an early hour...hanged together at 2:40 A.M. DST by official executioner John Ellis of Ottawa under the supervision of Sheriff John MacPhee. ... Pronounced dead by jail physician Dr. D. J. McGuire at 3:30 this morning...large numbers gathered outside for the death watch...."

It was over. I was free. And even though I'd gone to see them in those final days, and been assured they had no intention of involving me, I must admit I was glad when I read of their deaths. They could not touch me now.

Oh, I'd been nervous when I went to the Queen's County Jail. I didn't want to face them, but I had to. Can you understand that? I could not let them die without seeing them again, without thanking them for not involving me, without absorbing and admitting my guilt, without seeking forgiveness.

The conversation with them was short, pointed. They were on two kitchen chairs in the jailer's quarters, a guard, Ivan "Tinker" Martin, relaxing against the wall as we sat facing each other.

"Why did you say nothing?" I said to Frankie.

There was a long drawn-out pause as he studied me, finally smiling for his unseen audience, acting the big brother.

"There seemed no point. I ain't a squealer."

We sat in silence for a while.

"Ev?"

"You miserable little shit."

He spoke without emphasis, not mad, just reacting. I looked at Frankie. He inclined his head.

"Ev'll do what I say. We won't crack."

More silence. There was nothing to say. I looked at Frankie. "I'm sorry... about everything.... So...thanks, Frankie."

He nodded.

I looked at Ev. "Thanks, Ev."

"And to hell with you, too," he muttered, and laughed bitterly.

That was it. I left, escorted by Tinker.

"He's not at himself," the peace-loving Tinker explained by way of apology for Ev.

"I can understand that," I said.

✳ PART II

CHAPTER 14

When I look back to the time following the hangings, I remember it as a time of relaxation for the police, as a time of flagging spirits for the people, even as it was a time of apprehension and fear for me.

Murder, someone has written, transforms everything. Murders are exciting events that give people a sense of buoyancy. They come alive, make love with renewed vigour, finger their rosaries with greater reverence, are truly grateful to God for their lives, no matter how impoverished. As well, murders act as benchmarks to a community, reference points, much as a mother uses the birthdates of her children to trace events.

Emily Kate was much on my mind and in my thoughts at that time, and during that period of stress I think we grew closer. She told me of her new job offer from the Island Telephone Company, and I encouraged her to take it. She said she was sure she would.

I was muscling out nicely, like a lobster molting, growing...except in the heart. Except in the heart, where there remained a coldness combined with a persistent longing for something, I knew not what, but I associated it with Emily Kate. She often tried to get me to talk about myself, to open up, but I pushed these efforts aside with a laugh or silence. "There's nothing to talk about," I said. "What you see is what I am."

"You're deeper than that," she said, patting my cheek. "There's something bothering you. Unless you learn to open up you'll never grow."

I laughed, deliberately misunderstanding her. "Feel that muscle."

"That's not what I mean, and you know it."

She was the big sister, and I wanted more than that. We were in the front room of her boarding house, and I could hear the MacDonalds shuffling about upstairs. I contrasted the quietness, the calmness of this house with the chaos of my boarding house, the intensity of our lives there, the extremity of our emotions.

I grabbed Emily Kate and forced her back on the couch.

"Okay, so you have muscles. Let me up."

I forced my lips onto hers, pressed my body against hers. She kissed me back, but it was brief, and then she pushed me away.

"It's only a little kiss," I said.

"You'd want more."

"Is there anything wrong with wanting more?"

"You don't fool me. I'm no Mae Costello."

"I didn't think you were."

"Yes you did."

"You got me wrong, Emily Kate."

"I got you exactly right."

"Well, I'm sorry if I hurt your feelings," I said.

"You're not sorry. It's the way you treat all girls."

"How would you know?"

"I hear things."

Of course. I could see her in Ray's, listening in on the conversations, getting an education.

"I guess Ray's is as good a place as any to learn the facts of life," I said.

"I know the facts of life."

"And I know that bunch that hang around Ray's."

"As I said before, they're gentlemen compared to some."

"I know they've been trying to get into your knickers."

I couldn't be satisfied with one foot in my mouth, I had to try for a regiment.

"Charming...so you thought you'd beat them to it?"

"No, I—"

"You thought they'd succeeded?"

"No."

"They hadn't."

"I knew that."

"You should have."

I sat down beside her, touching her arm tentatively. She moved her arm away.

"There's just one thing I have to say to you," I said.

"What's that?"

"You know," I said, the words coming hard, "you must know...that no one will ever...love you...as I do."

She dropped her eyes. "Is that a...proposal?"

"What?"

"Are you asking me to marry you?"

"I...uh...well...." My voice trailed off and she let me dangle.

"That's what I thought. That means I don't have to refuse you."

"Would you?"

"You haven't asked, so you'll never know. Anyway, you're too young."

"Damn it, Emily Kate, stop playing games."

"You! You have the nerve to accuse me of playing games?"

"I just meant—"

"Never mind. I don't want to hear it. It'd just be another one of your lies. You'd better go now."

I put my tail between my legs and left. There was no goodbye, nothing tender. I could see that the kiss meant nothing to her, and this was confirmed over the next while. When I phoned, she was curt or hung up, often in the middle of a conversation. I couldn't figure her out.

*

I was by now full-time at the *Patriot.* And as I covered stories around town, feeling the emptiness of Emily Kate's loss, I wandered the city streets, absorbing the aura, picking up nuances. Nothing was what it seemed. The morning businessmen, sweeping their sidewalks, cleaning their windows, displayed the false joviality of the opportunist hoping to ensnare passing pedestrians into their lairs. They paid obeisance to the master, Chester R. Ross, as he paraded each day from his home in Brighton, tall, smiling, in his vicuna coat with the velvet lapels, to his downtown clothing emporium, strategically located on the border of the business district between the world of commerce and the world of poverty, catching in his bargain basement the poor, those whose need for clothing was matched by the lack of means to purchase it, his main floor accommodating the upscale, those with disposable income.

Chester R. was a large, friendly man, open, generous, with a kind word for everybody. He never missed a sporting event, he was liked and admired by all, and his credit slips would have revealed that he placed his trust in people not in their material standing, his accounts in the poorer parts of town as numerous as those elsewhere. Witness his being asked and agreeing to serve as a pallbearer for Peter Hogan; it was not the custom of the time for Catholics to have Protestant pallbearers, or vice versa, and here was Chester R. Ross, a Protestant leader in the city, not only attending, but kneeling and praying at the Requiem Mass for his old customer and friend.

I jotted notes to describe the whole picture: the streets busy with struggling horses hauling the two-wheeled, compact, high dump carts that held exactly one ton of coal; the delivery jiggers with their low flat beds lying close to the street for ease of lifting goods on and off; more and more cars and trucks, and now and then the show team of eight ponderous Percherons from Simon Paoli's Lumber Yard, much bedecked in bright ribbons, the sun reflecting from the shining brasses, parading through the city, proudly guided by the expert hands of a beaming Peter Pineau, the earth-shaking thudding of their heavy hooves spelling doom for any wayward sparrow caught feasting on street droppings.

And when I mention old Chester R. Ross walking to work past the admiring glances of others, I should more accurately tell about them letting down their awnings, dressing their windows, preparing for customers: Henry Peters of the Queen Street Meat Market, in white apron, hosing out his shop and the sidewalk in front; the three Dougan sisters fussing in their women's wear window; the Hardy Brothers, harness and luggage merchants, who always seemed old, dusting off the horse collars and harness and bags which seemed on permanent display in their shop on the corner across from City Hall; their harness-maker and repairman, Joe Bradley, paying homage to no man, ensconced in his little shop around the corner on Kent Street, always willing to take a few stitches in a battered baseball, or a glove, or a hockey gauntlet, always with a kind word and a smile for kids, but otherwise dry and taciturn; Ches Campbell smoking in the doorway of his tiny jewellery shop next to Fennell and Chandler's Hardware Store; lanky Tom White across the street in front of his restaurant, waving at passers-by with his ever present cigar; and the kids, particularly on Saturdays and after school, weaving in and out among the adults uptown, ripping through the Five-and-Ten or the Metropolitan with shoplifted items of little value, flashing glances over their shoulders to assess the measure of the pursuit, disappearing into the crowd, or into another store, or into a gangway.

Kids learned the backyard routes out of trouble. I recalled my school days when Mr. Stacey, the manager of the

Five-and-Ten, complained to Queen Square School principal, Leo F. MacDonald, about the light-fingered tendencies of his students. Mr. MacDonald laid down the law: keep out of the Five-and-Ten unless accompanied by a parent or an adult.

Since he was a well-respected principal, the law was obeyed — for a month. Then, in one fell swoop, about ten youngsters, caps low on their heads, drifted into the store in ones and twos, gathered at the back, and swept forward, grabbing at anything that wasn't nailed down, hitting the front door like a wave, up the street, in behind the Prince Edward Theatre, over the fence by Ford's Blacksmith Shop, behind Bill Chaisson's house, into Wally Scantlebury's upper yard where the City kept its horses, down past Tommy Holmes's tiny dwelling, across Kent Street, through Frank Bell's garden, over the fence into John Black's yard, where, under the plum trees, the loot was divided, the toys and the rest, and especially the candy and even a jar of doughnuts and an apple pie grabbed off the lunch counter, rapidly split up and devoured on the spot.

Innocence prevailed the next day. An assembly was called, Mr. Stacey paraded up and down the aisle trying to identify the culprits, but, confronted with only grins from the sea of faces, he turned to the principal with a shrug, a sad smile, a shake of his head. He gave a little speech and did not, as expected, warn us to stay out of his store. He said that Queen Square boys were always welcome in the Five-and-Ten. From that day on, the store was let alone and breaches were swiftly and unmercifully dealt with by the boys themselves. When Sniffy O'Neill — whose dripping proboscis posed an altogether different problem than that afflicting a colleague named Snotty-Nose Haggerty — when Sniffy foolishly displayed his courage by twice disregarding the code, he had two fingers broken, one on each hand, as well as his nose. His parents, wiser than Sniffy, took him out of Queen Square

— "a bunch of barbarians" — and enrolled him in West Kent School down by Government Pond where he actually did quite well among the Protestant boys and girls — to the point where we came to envy him his good fortune. He even thanked his violators for the nose-break, patting it fondly, remarking that for whatever reason it no longer dripped.

But such is the power of nicknames on the Island, that when he died some forty years on, his obituary in the paper that "covers Prince Edward Island like the dew" was headed O'NEILL, Lawrence Edward (Sniffy). I'm hoping I outlive HAGGERTY, John James to see how they handle that one.

❊

Jokes sprang up about Frankie Hanlan in the morbid way that people have. Frankie, they said, had always spoken highly about loyalty and favoured the direct approach. "I'd like you to be loyal," he supposedly said to Ev Noonan, "or else I'll break your goddam neck."

In a story about the now-armed police, the wags told about the cop who went to Confession and confessed that he'd shot at Frankie Hanlan.

"And did you hit him, my son?" the priest asked.

"No, Father, I missed."

"For your Penance, say the Rosary five times, then try again for the son-of-a-bitch."

People will nail you when you're down — or dead.

CHAPTER 15

I used to be afraid of the press, but of one thing I was always certain: the press had power. The words were synonymous in my mind. "In olden days men had the rack," Oscar Wilde said. "Now they have the press." And Peter Finley Dunne said, "The press...rules by finding out what the people want, and if they don't want anything, it tells them what it wants them to tell it they want."

So whether the press was guilty of monopoly, of government control, of timidity in the face of corporate pressure, of a big business mentality, of social blindness, or whether the press was capable of being the instrument used to elevate man to the highest point of which his faculties admit, of serving as a forum for the people through which they might know freely what is going on, the truth was that at that time the press was the most powerful force in the world.

Can you even partly begin to understand my avidity to become associated with this behemoth? I was eager and anxious to prostrate myself at its feet.

As my situation changed, I wondered if I would change with it. Yes, I decided, the answer was yes. Perhaps all identification is temporary since a person goes through a lifetime of changing situations, and therefore we become many different people over the course of years. This seemed to me a very satisfying theory, and I gradually worked myself to the conclusion that now was the time for a change of name. I'd been Mickey Corcoran long enough.

I went to the Department of Vital Statistics where Jack MacAleer briefed me on the procedure with forms to be completed and notices placed in the *Royal Gazette*. I decided to take my mother's name of Casey, added the Christian name of Hugh after a man who'd been kind to me in the orphanage (the janitor, Hughie Somers), and gave myself the respectable Irish name of Michael, which I later learned was Hebrew, but never mind. I liked the rhythm of Hugh Michael Casey, and made it official. Of course, I still get Mickey and probably always will, but Corcoran has all but been forgotten. I hear "Old Man Casey" the odd time, or "H. M.," or, even at times, spitefully, "His Majesty."

The change, unfortunately, did not include any cutback on my drinking, which, in rare moments of candour, I admitted to myself was becoming a problem.

CHAPTER 16

When you're busy trying to advance in a tough business, time passes rapidly. I was gaining experience, covering all kinds of stories, contributing occasional feature articles and the odd by-lined opinion piece for the editorial page. Over a period of months, this latter, like Pinocchio's nose, "just grew and grew," until readers came to expect it, and I was given a weekly column.

This did wonders for my confidence and also meant a few more dollars in my pocket. But most of all, the parameters of a column allowed me liberties forbidden by a news story. Opinion, conjecture, rumour — almost anything short of libel was grist for the columnist's mill. I loved this new-found freedom.

Emily Kate, too, was doing well in her new job at the Island Telephone Company. In a matter of months, she had gone from being a "Number please" girl to supervisor of operators. I saw her off and on, but it was casual only. She let me know that she was off-limits.

"C'mon, Emily Kate, a little kiss. We're friends, aren't we?"

"You and Billy are friends. Kiss him."

"It's not quite the same," I observed drily.

"There'll be none of that until I hear something about commitment."

"C'mon, Emily Kate, loosen up. It's what friends do."

"Not this friend. Get your cheap thrills someplace else."

It was not like that all the time, thank God, or I might have thrown in the towel. Every now and then she let me experience the depth of her passion, but always with the good sense to rein herself — and me — in at the crucial moment.

These were moments I lived for. I always considered them almost like a bonus for good behaviour. But mainly our dates — if you could call them that — ended on a sour note. We seemed to function in a state of permanent animosity.

Billy Williams seemed to have found his niche at Dooley's Dairy, where he had advanced from working a route, to route chief, then to an inside job as route supervisor. By the time he became plant manager, he had grown into a burly, crew-cut hard case, and the word was that he ruled the plant with his fists. Billy took his civic duty seriously and won a seat on the City Council on his first try. There were those who hinted that he had threatened reprisals in his Ward if he didn't win, but there was no way to prove rumours like that. And to top it all, within a year of his last promotion, the word was out that Billy was now the major shareholder in the dairy, although there was no official announcement to that effect.

When Emily Kate called Billy my friend she was stretching the truth, and she knew it. We were never really friends, even in our orphanage days, and I had no desire to get closer. Emily Kate, Billy, and I were a group of three set apart because of our shared experiences, but Billy and I were only acquaintances. In fact, I had already written a column hinting at improprieties at City Hall — without naming anyone, just suggesting that perhaps matters should be looked into. I knew, too, that Billy was crazy about Emily Kate and this, as much as anything, made him a target for me.

It came as a surprise then when Billy invited me to lunch with himself and Emily Kate.

"What's the occasion?" I asked.

"Nothing. Just thought the three of us could get together."

I knew that Billy didn't do anything without a reason. This probably had something to do with my recent column, I thought. The newspaperman's creed: give no credit without proof and then hedge because there is always — always — a hidden agenda.

But my curiosity was aroused.

"Fine," I said, and we agreed on a time and place. I added, "Celebrating your majority shareholder status?"

There was a pause, then Billy laughed. "There's nothing to that story," he said.

I had no idea what this lunch would bring, only that I hoped it would somehow give me a sign about how things stood with Billy and Emily Kate, and perhaps let me press home my own case with her — that, compared with Billy, I would come off well.

At the lunch, she avoided speaking pointedly to me, directing her remarks into space.

"Pass the pepper, please," she aimed at the back wall, and I obliged.

"I can't go anywhere next Sunday," she told the passing waitress in reply to my invitation.

"Yes, work is going well," she said directly into Billy's eyes to answer my query.

It wasn't a comfortable meal.

"Am I invisible — or what?" I asked.

Billy laughed. "Why would you say that?"

"Things keep missing me."

"What are you talking about?"

"Remarks bounce off the wall, or over my head, or into my plate. It's like I'm not here."

"You seem real enough to me."

"It's not you I mean, Billy."

"Oh, you mean Emily Kate," he said. "She is quiet, isn't she? But then she always was. Remember those times down in the orchard?"

Emily Kate spoke after a period of silence.

"Those were times when we all trusted each other,

weren't they?"

Ah, I realized. I had poisoned the well with my column, and I was being punished.

"What do you mean?" I asked.

"Just that. We did not then suspect betrayal in each other, did we?"

So help me, that's what she said: "suspect betrayal."

"It's not betrayal to speak the truth," I said.

"The truth? *Your* truth, you mean. No facts, just innuendo — hinting at something wrong."

"Billy can prove he's not guilty if he's done nothing wrong."

"Of course he can, but why should he? Proving a negative — it's like trying to prove you don't beat your wife."

"Hey, hey," Billy interrupted. "Take it easy, you two. Don't talk about me like I'm not here."

He patted Emily Kate's hand. "It's nothing personal with Mickey."

I glared at him. I knew he was just trying to look good in Emily Kate's eyes.

"I'm glad you understand that," I said coldly. "Can you tell me one thing, Billy — what was the purpose of this meeting?"

His broad face was bland, but he'd never win an Academy Award.

"Purpose? just like I said, to get together, to chat."

"Yeah."

"I have to get back to work," Billy said, shoving out of the booth. "I'll get the cheque. Good to see you again, Mickey. Maybe we can do this more often."

As he moved away, he gave a low chuckle. I felt my cheeks and neck burning.

"Blushing?" she said. "That's not like you."

"Can you tell me what's going on here, Emily Kate?"

Now she stared directly into my eyes, holding me transfixed as only she could.

"Billy's had word that you're investigating him."

"So that's what this is about. 'Investigating's' a little strong. I'm looking into rumours, checking out reports that have come my way."

"Why do you attack him on the basis of rumours?"

"I'm not attacking him."

"You're slanting your reports."

"I'm very careful not to do that."

I was, in fact, trying carefully to slant the stories regarding activities on City Council in such a way that they appeared as objective as possible, but hinting at blame. But Emily Kate was not the casual reader, at least as far as Billy Williams was concerned.

"Then what does this mean?" She pulled a clipping from her purse and read: "'Word on the street is that the Mayor has invited the City Police to look into suspected irregularities regarding a recent land deal.' What about that?"

"What about it? It's true — they're looking into it."

"They weren't until your column appeared."

"That's not what my source says."

"Your source!" The contempt was obvious. "You knew this would lead to Billy since he's the Chair of the Land Committee."

I opened my hands and shrugged in a what-can-I-do gesture. "If Billy's innocent he's got nothing to fear."

The green eyes were flashing. "You are a bastard. Here's something else for your rumour column: word on the street is that I'm going to marry Billy."

I slumped back as if hit with a baseball bat, and I felt my insides turn to water. There is a wall, a frontier of the emotions, where one feels compelled to surrender self-possession, dignity, maturity, and abandon oneself wholly to grief. Such moments occur often at funerals when the sense of loss of a loved one finally strikes home. This was such a moment for me.

I sat there stupidly shaking my head.

There was triumph in her eyes.

"No," I said, wiping a hand across my face. "You can't do this, Emily Kate."

"Yes, I can. And I will."

"But...but...."

"Yes?"

"But...I love you."

"I understand that," she said, and even in my stricken state I realized her voice had gentled somewhat. "But what does that mean?"

"It...it...means I...love you," I stammered.

"And?"

And I couldn't continue. I just couldn't. I could not take that final irreparable step. Within me, in the Bermuda Triangle of my soul, the finer feelings of love and tenderness shrivelled and disappeared into the raging sea and left me empty. I lowered my head onto my arms, my eyes hidden.

"That's what I thought," she said. "Goodbye, Mickey."

I remained as I was, silent, too ashamed to raise my eyes to hers.

✳

I had not visited the orphanage since I'd left it all those years ago, but no sooner had I taken a deep breath inside the front door than I was back again, seized by the feeling of loss I had known there.

The Mother Superior was the same nun — older, greyer, more haggard, but with all her senses intact.

"The Lord has given me a vision," she declared, throwing wide her arms. "It's the grand Michael himself — or my eyes deceive me."

I smiled as we hugged. "You're still twenty-twenty, Mother."

"I hear good things about you," she said. "Shall we kill the fatted calf, or, in our case, a scrawny hen?"

"No need, Mother, I'm just here for a few minutes. Got a taxi waiting."

She sobered. "Very well, then. Why do I get the feeling that this has something to do with Emily Kate?"

"Right again," I said. "Look, Mother, I don't know how to put this, and I'm not looking to breach confidences, but I'm anxious to find out anything that happened to Emily Kate after I left."

She could easily have said, "You left it long enough," but she didn't.

"So long ago," she murmured. "Find out what?"

"Well...like how did she behave? Did she miss me? Did she and Billy Williams become friends? Like that."

"I suppose I can tell you, since it was common knowledge, that for the first few weeks after you left she was inconsolable, always waiting for you to return, if only for a visit."

The way she looked at me was chastisement enough.

"She finally accepted that you weren't coming back. And that's when she turned to Billy. Now, it's no news to you that Billy was and still is a bully, but the devil his due, I can say truthfully that he always treated Emily Kate with respect, and protected her from others who would have taken advantage of her."

My heart sank as I listened to her words. "It's true then."

"What's true?"

"I think they're going to be married," I said.

She reached out and touched my arm.

"I'm sorry, Michael. I'm truly sorry if you've lost her to Billy Williams. I think you'd be the better man for her."

I smiled my thanks as I left. If she could have seen into

my heart just then, she would have retracted her remarks, because at the hard core inside me where I lived, Billy Williams's fate had been sealed.

✳

Three months later, William J. Williams and Emily Kate Ryan were married in St. Dunstan's Basilica, with a small reception afterwards at the Charlottetown Hotel. I was invited, but declined to answer or attend. I did, however, send a gift, a serving bowl, a fine and handsome piece of Waterford crystal that I'd bought for what I'd hoped would be an engagement gift when I one day asked Emily Kate to marry me. I had no further use for it.

Emily Kate was not stupid. She must have known Billy was not all he pretended to be. She must have had suspicions. Yet I can see into her mind, and I know she was thinking that she could change him. People always spoke of the influence of a good woman, and Emily Kate knew she was that. What she didn't realize was that she was dealing no longer with a child, but with an adult, and, in Billy's case, with a particularly obstinate adult, one to whom malleability was a stranger, one already going in the only direction he knew. He would be tender with her, kind, until the time came when she inquired too deeply into his affairs, questioned too persistently his actions or his motives, then the bully would reassert himself. Of this I was sure, but such reflections did me no good on that wedding day.

I spent the day with a bottle of John Jameson's, engaging in a battle often fought, seldom won. On my way to oblivion, I saw, with the added clarity provided by the whiskey, the simplicity of the task before me: to ruin Billy Williams without appearing to do so. Billy was the burr under my saddle, the canker in my mouth, the gnawing headache that wouldn't go away.

I thought of the direct approach I'd used to destroy the Costello brothers in ten seconds of violent action, but discarded that method at once. That was fine for the fire of youth, but this would have to be more subtle. I tucked the problem into the back of my mind, knowing that, as always, my subconscious would work on it, and the solution would surface in its own good time. It didn't seem to require much more than simply following my present path.

Was I a monster? Of course not. I considered myself a spurned suitor, entitled to Emily Kate. I was convinced I was her one true love with the right to do whatever it took to win her back.

Was I crazy? Completely amoral? I thought not. I had given up on most of the trappings of Catholicism, true, but I still felt a spirituality that kept me within striking distance of a Higher Power. The two murders for which I was responsible seemed not only entirely justifiable, but almost to be from another lifetime.

I was only too well aware of Billy's reputation for brutality and ruthlessness. In my drunken stupour, I smiled. I'd give him ruthless. The abiding thought I carried into unconsciousness was the rightness of my cause.

Good fortune smiled on me two days later when, still suffering the whips and jingles of a hangover, I had a visit at the paper from Joe "Bull" Harrigan, who wanted to tell me about how he lost his job at Dooley's Dairy. The Bull was cut from the same cloth as Billy Williams: broad, burly, hard-fisted. But he had a strange story to tell, and he told it well — a tale of intrigue, bullying, and suspected blackmail that cured my lingering headache in moments.

Bull had no proof, but plenty of circumstantial evidence, the kind that more often than not escalated into a court case.

When he finished, he sat there watching me scribbling

my last few notes.

"Can you use any of that?" he asked.

"Maybe."

"I want my name kept out of it."

"That's fine with me. I can always quote 'a source close to the top.'"

Bull sneered. "The son-of-a-bitch'll never suspect me. He'd never think of me as close to the top."

"Tell me, Bull, why do you think old man Dooley was blackmailed?"

"He came to me after I was fired. After all, I was there eighteen years. The old man knew me well."

"And?"

"And he gave me my severance bonus. Said we'd both been done in by the same bastard. I didn't put much stock in it at the time — too sorry for myself. But when I thought about it later, it seemed the only way Williams could have got control so fast. I was you, I'd have a word with George O'Brien as well."

"Why?"

"He was the other one who sold out and made Williams the major shareholder."

I had my first religious thought in ages. It was, "The Lord has delivered Billy Williams into my hands." I had a hard time hiding my glee. This was going to be a lovely mess to dig into, and I was giddy with the thought of having the bold Billy on my spit.

"Can you feel it?" I asked Bull Harrigan.

"Feel what?"

"The electricity in the air."

"I don't feel nothing."

"Bull, Bull, they say that in the seconds before lightning strikes, you can feel everything around you buzzing. Can't you feel it now?"

He looked at me strangely. "Naw."

"It's there, it's there. And I think that lightning is about to strike Billy Williams."

That he understood, and he left the office beaming.

I dwelt on it a few moments longer. For people like me who've had to fight for everything, there are few things in life equal to the satisfaction that comes from well-planned retaliation. He took Emily Kate from me, I would take something from him. To my mind, it was simply a case of *quid pro quo*, a Roland for an Oliver, an eye for an eye, and a tooth for a tooth. I knew Billy would understand; anybody raised in an orphanage would. Nothing is ever handed to us as our family due, there are no parental bouquets, nothing is tossed our way as a right. Lesson One: You get what you earn. Lesson Two: If you can't earn it, take it anyway. Lesson Three: There is nothing easy about life; smile and be a villain. Lesson Four (and most important): Don't get caught.

Billy Williams was about to learn that he had not taken enough precautions to avoid the most important lesson.

CHAPTER 17

In sane moments, I pondered the smoothness of language, and I decried the lack of grace when I heard David Brinkley, mind you a young David Brinkley, say: "In the end McCarthy having never ever found even one Communist not already known, the whiskey got to him and he died of cirrhosis of the liver." I studied Lord Macaulay as a model to help my prose style, admiring the regularity, uniformity, precision, and balance of his sentences, his clarity and terseness, sparing of ornament and pomposity, so sensitive as to be positively numinous, filling me to overflowing with jealous admiration.

I went through a manic phase where I saw things — a cat, a bird, a hurtling car — not directly, but out of the corner of my eye, on the periphery of vision, no more than a swift dark movement, a floater in my sideways glance. I wrote furiously at these times, usually destroying it all later.

More than once, I found I was a writer who couldn't write, but I knew that was not unusual. Oh, I got by the day-to-day reporting with the formula, the who, what, where, when, and why, but any depth was lacking. I could not give any flesh to the bones, and I often lacked slant. I know a journalist is supposed to be objective, give just the facts, not impose any slant, but in my view, objectivity is overrated. What a good reporter is always trying to do is to inject opinion into his piece in such a way that the reader is unaware of what he's doing.

The world of the journalist and the world of the historian are not far removed from each other. Oscar Wilde said that the proper occupation of the historian is to give an accurate description of what has never occurred, and while that may be taking things a bit far, as Wilde was wont to do, it is fair to say that one can be too sanctimonious about objectivity, and reporters I knew avoided the use of the word and its meaning as well.

Not to put too fine a point on it, the world I was dealing with was of the common, ordinary, garden variety: sporting events, car and train wrecks, school honour rolls, political meetings; meetings of the Knights of Pythias, the Knights of Columbus, the Women's Institutes, and the CWL; but with plenty of leeway in my column to question possible intrigue and shady events that otherwise would never have received any public airing.

The everyday things, as minuscule and unimportant as they were, were occurring simultaneously with events in the secret, hidden world of evil about which nothing could be written because, by consent of all, such a world did not exist — at least not in the Charlottetown of the day.

But I could hint at it.

The paper had threats of lawsuits because of my writing, but nothing ever materialized, although to be honest I was often worried and spent many sleepless nights because I knew how much I'd twisted stories, and I wondered if anyone would finally have the nerve to call me.

Especially I worried about Billy, but neither his nor anyone else's charges ever ended up in court.

✻

Digging into Billy's past at the dairy to figure out how he obtained control so quickly was not as daunting as I first thought. My main problem was how to approach old Dan Dooley to make it appear a casual encounter.

I leisurely trailed him for a few days and found that he visited the Gentlemen's Club regularly about 11:30 each morning. I waited there one day and as he got out of his car, I got out of mine.

"Mr. Dooley," I said. "How are you, sir?"

"You look familiar, young man. Do I know you?"

"Michael Casey, sir. At the *Patriot.*"

"Ah, yes, I've seen your face on your column often enough. You write good stuff, young man, most of the time anyway."

"Thank you, sir."

Now, I thought, can I slip one by him?

"I was wondering, sir, if you could help me with a story I'm working on?"

He looked me over carefully. "Our meeting is no accident, I take it?"

Sharp old bugger. I smiled sheepishly. "Not exactly, sir."

"What is it you want?"

"It's like this, Mr. Dooley. I'm looking into Billy Williams, and I heard from a reliable source that there was something irregular about his quick rise at the dairy."

There. It was out in the open. I have found in this work that the direct approach is the best. Beat around the bush, and people suspect you. Better to make your case cleanly. If they're going to turn you down, they'll turn you down anyway, no matter how you pussyfoot around it.

"A reliable source, eh?"

"Yes sir."

"I don't suppose you could say who that is?"

"No sir, definitely not."

Fast and emphatic. By doing this you hope to pass on a sense of security to your interviewee, the implication that you'll do the same for him.

I was aware of our long silence, of birds chirping in the trees across the street by the Bishop's Residence, of traffic along Great George Street.

He looked at me warily. "How much do you know about this business?"

"Quite a bit, Mr. Dooley." Never admit that you know

next to nothing.

"Come inside with me and have a drink."

Seated in big easy chairs with our drinks, he seemed more in command.

"Again, now, what is your purpose here?"

"Only one thing, sir. If something crooked went on, I'd like to know about it. We already know," I said to pry him open a little, "about Billy's shady actions at City Hall."

He raised his brows. "There, too?"

"Oh yes. It seems to be part of Billy's nature."

"I don't want any reference to myself — none whatsoever."

"No sir, that's a given. Nor will there be any to George O'Brien."

Again, the raised brows. "You *do* know quite a lot."

I just smiled, and he began. He told me in a guarded way of some indiscretion years ago, and how Billy convinced the young lady involved to write a very damning letter which would have ruined Dooley's home life, if nothing else.

"Had it been a few years earlier," he mused, "I would have handled it myself and thrown both Williams and the inventive young lady off the bridge. But...I just couldn't put my wife through that."

I looked at those big-knuckled hands and that craggy determined face, and suffered a moment of admiration for Billy Williams for daring to beard this old lion in his den.

"Oh, we got a fair price, George and I. Billy went to the bank with intent-to-sell letters from us both, and had no trouble raising the money."

"So — it was blackmail."

"Absolutely not. I hate that word."

"Don't worry, Mr. Dooley, I won't use it. This information will be handled very judiciously."

He sat back more relaxed. "You know," he said, "I've

thought about it often over the years, and I often wish I'd stood up to the bastard. There would've been a few hard months, and then it would've been over. But...I always come back to it, it would probably have killed my wife. It doesn't seem to matter so much anymore — she died a year ago."

I already knew this — was counting on it, in fact.

"I'm sorry," I said.

"You won't be getting corroboration from George O'Brien. He's dead, too."

"Yes. I knew that."

"But he left me a full notarized statement of what happened to him — if you can use that information discreetly as well."

I chuckled. "That's a bonus, Mr. Dooley. Thanks a lot."

"Nothing can hurt George now," he said. "And there's damn little that matters to me anymore."

He rose, and so did I. He stuck out his hand, and I shook it.

"Get the bastard," he said.

✳

I needed some time to assimilate all this, and I needed also to do more digging into the City Hall story. I had a number of contacts there, and I called one of them now — warty-faced Stan Baldwin, a minor clerk in the main office, mousy and silent, who crept around the levers of power as if invisible. No one ever remembered seeing Stan anywhere. He was an ideal mole.

"Can't give you anything, Mickey," he said. "But I can tell you who to talk to."

"Yeah?"

"John McCormack — he lost the sand-hauling contract."

"God Almighty, Stan, are you on another planet? I'm talking about the land deal for the new city dump."

"I know. Here's what you don't know. John's wife's sister is married to Charlie Robinson."

"Hold on a minute," I said as I processed this information. Charlie was the one who sold the land to the city. He'd tell his wife who would talk to her sister. The sister would tell her husband, John McCormack, who'd be pissed off that Charlie got the deal while he, John, had lost out on his. And he just might be willing to spill the beans about his brother-in-law.

"Got it," I said.

"You're slowing down in your old age, Mickey."

"Ain't we all? Thanks, Stan."

"Anytime. Keep me out of it."

"Naturally."

"Don't see you at Freedie's much lately."

"I'll be there Saturday night. Drinks on me."

"You got that right," he said.

✳

When liquored up, John McCormack talked like a hyped-up neurotic. He knew I worked at the *Patriot*, but here, in Freedie's, I was just a fellow drinker. I steered the conversation onto happenings in the city.

"What about that new dump?" I said. "I bet that piece of land went for quite a price."

"Goddam son of a bitch."

"Pardon me?"

"Billy Williams. He got a kickback."

"How much?"

"Ten thousand."

I laughed. "Get out of here. How would you know that, John?"

He was stung by my laughter. "I goddam well know it."

"But how?"

"The wife told me. Her sister's married to Charlie Robinson."

"Ten thousand?"

"That's what she said."

"Must be true then."

"And the bastard wouldn't even give me the sand-hauling contract, even though I promised him a cut."

"Yeah?"

"Yeah. Said he got a bigger cut from Matt Crumley."

More bonuses coming my way.

"How much?" I asked.

"How would I know? I offered him a thousand. Maybe two or three, something like that."

"Billy's doing all right on the side," I said.

"The bastard. I hope he drops dead. It's getting so an ordinary decent crook can't make a living no more in this city."

"It's a goddam shame," I said. "Have another drink, John?"

"Goddam right."

✳

Revenge is a kind of wild justice. I have never subscribed to Solomon's dictum, that it is the glory of a man to pass by an offence. Hell, even Solomon himself didn't. We are commanded to forgive our enemies, sometimes an easy task, but you never read that we are commanded to forgive our friends, an infinitely more difficult task, and one I never mastered.

> *The villas and the chapels*
> *Where I learned with little labour,*
> *The way to love my fellow-man,*
> *And hate my next-door neighbour.*

A man who studies revenge keeps his own wounds green, and my body was a mass of suppurating sores as I habitually dwelt over offences, real and imagined. This kind of thinking feeds on itself, leading to what? Paranoia? Madness?

Billy Williams thinks I hate him. He's right!

I was able to lend my black motives the external sheen of good deeds and for a time escape self-recrimination.

Just as the greatest virtue is charity, the willingness to lay down one's life for another, so also the greatest evil must be murder, the taking of another's life.

And while my dark soul seemed to cry out for this greatest act, my wiser self backed off from it and settled on destroying Billy Williams, until gradually the possibility of destruction became the necessity of destruction. I had finally reached what Shakespeare called the point where the two prayers cross, where, in the human heart, good and evil are created in the one gesture, meld, and become one.

I called Billy Williams. He invited me to meet him in his boardroom at the dairy, and, while it is not my practice to meet the enemy on the field of his choice, I was so smug in the cards I held that I agreed.

The rich, sweet, milky odour of a working dairy engulfed me as I entered, taking me back to my days as Mickey Corker, and the time I passed the job along to Billy. Light splashed on his desk from the south windows. I missed the rattle and bang of bottles from the past. Now it was all plastic bags and cartons.

The niceties passed quickly. Billy was the same height as me — six feet — but heavier. Not fat, hard. The greying crew cut, the hard planes of his face, the light-blue innocent eyes — many a man to his sorrow had failed to see the steel beneath. His suit pulled tight across his massive shoulders. I had to remind myself that this was not the Billy Williams I'd known at the orphanage, but a deadlier one who had faced down old Dan Dooley.

Billy, too, believed in the direct approach. "Still digging into my affairs?"

"There's so much to find."

"You know, Mickey, I'da thought you'd be more filled with a sense of solidarity — you know, you, me, Emily Kate — we made something of ourselves."

"And how is Emily Kate?"

"Fine. She got another promotion."

"I hear she's working out of Halifax now."

"Yeah, temporary. Home on the weekends. Not the best, but she'll quit one of these days and stay home."

"I doubt it," I said.

I got the hard blank stare.

"What would you know about it?"

"Very little. I just think that Emily Kate has a strong desire to succeed on her own."

The eyes went dull. "She don't have to work."

"I know that, Billy. What with all the dough you got rolling in, probably neither of you'd have to work another day."

"What does that mean?"

"Just that. What with a controlling interest in the dairy, and your city council benefits...."

The eyes went suspicious.

"Billy," I said, "does the word 'blackmail' mean anything to you?"

"You got a big mouth, you know that? Why don't you just spit it out."

"Okay. I know all about you blackmailing Dan Dooley and George O'Brien. I know about your cut on the land deal with Charlie Robinson. I know about your cut on the hauling contract with Matt Crumley. I know — well, hell, Billy, you get the idea. How'm I doing so far?"

He sat calmly through it all. Then he rose slowly, reached across his desk, caught the front of my clothes and hauled me to within six inches of his face. The muscles in his jaw hardened.

"If you print so much as one word of that," he spat at me, "I'll sue the arse off you and that rag, then I'll kill you."

"Easy, Billy, take it easy."

He threw me back into my seat. I sat, rearranging my clothes as he collected his wits.

"That's all lies anyway," he said finally. "What we got here is a he-said, she-said situation."

"We got more than that, Billy. What we got here are affidavits."

He sat back, smiling, twirling a pencil. "You ain't got no affidavits."

It was my turn to smile. "Hold that thought, Billy."

He laughed, as if he knew I was bluffing.

"Wait'll I tell Emily Kate about this. She'll have your guts for garters. Now get out of here, I got work to do."

I didn't feel nearly as good as I thought I would. Will he try to brazen it out, I wondered, or will he come after me? Billy's bullying days were not behind him, and I knew the way a bully acts when he can't get what he wants.

CHAPTER 18

My concern about danger from Billy was ill-founded. When a bully is confronted, he'll do one of two things: lash out or run to home. Billy chose the latter, so I should not have been surprised to hear directly from Emily Kate. She called from Halifax, said she was coming over to Charlottetown and asked could she see me.

"No problem," I said. Then I laughed.

"What?"

"So Billy's getting you to throw his snowballs."

She ignored that, and we set a date for lunch the next day at the Charlottetown Hotel.

Because my experience with the Charlottetown Hotel goes back so far, I never enter it but I have a feeling of awe as I gaze around. Nothing much has changed. There've been renovations from time to time, of course, but the latest owner understands the necessity of preserving the past, so the front entrance and lobby would be readily recognized by a person re-registering after a fifty-year absence.

All male eyes in the room were on Emily Kate as she approached my table. She was wearing an olive-green suit that highlighted her red hair and green eyes. I shook my head in admiration as I rose to greet her, noting that fine-boned, slender, patrician grace that was the mark of refinement, achieved in Emily Kate's case, unwittingly, solely by instinct.

"I'm the envy of every man in the place," I said.

"It's good to see you, too," she said. We shook hands formally. It had been a long time since I'd seen her.

Lunch was fast, a bowl of chowder for her, a sandwich for me. During the small talk, I learned the following: the move to Halifax was permanent, not temporary, as Billy had said, but they'd "work something out"; the most recent promotion made her Director of Communications, a grand title for "a flack"; yes, she knew Jack Brady, he was "a good friend," and her immediate superior.

This gave me pause, but only for a moment. Jack was an old drinking buddy of mine and a good guy, but I also knew that since he was single he'd be interested in Emily Kate. Of course, I also knew her, and when she said he was "a good friend," she meant just that.

"And the paper?" she said. "I hear you're moving up."

I shrugged. "There's always news."

"Isn't that the truth?" she said, and neatly segued into, "And when there isn't, you manufacture it yourself."

I smiled. "That's one thing I don't do."

The gloves were off. We were like a divorcing couple across the table from each other. All we needed were the lawyers.

"What I do do," I added, "is fight my own battles."

Her gaze was level, tinged with contempt. "Billy wanted to come. In fact, he desperately wanted to be here. I had to insist it'd be better if I came alone."

"Probably wanted to beat the crap out of me."

"That thought crossed my mind."

She shifted in her seat, concentrating. The dining room noises around us, the rattle of dishes, receded into the background. There was only Emily Kate and me.

"You've not run the story yet," she said.

I shrugged. "Still gathering and checking."

That was a lie. I had, in fact, more than enough evidence to cause Billy Williams a lot of grief. What I was struggling with was the damage this might do to Emily Kate.

"You were never one to let the truth stand in the way of a good story," she said.

That stung. "I've got enough truth to hurt Billy."

She made a placating gesture, her hand continuing across the table to touch my hand for a moment. I felt my skin burn.

"Sorry," she said. "That was uncalled for."

"But true," I admitted ruefully, my feelings soothed by her apology. My God, one kind word, and I'm willing to lick her hand.

She shifted gears. "Things are going well at the paper?"

"As well as could be expected. And the flack business?"

"I find it easy to be positive about a company I enjoy working for."

"Yes...you would."

"What does that mean?"

"Oh, for God's sake, Emily Kate, I meant it as a compliment. I meant that you are a good person yourself and would see only the good in anything — or anybody."

"That's not true."

"Oh?"

"I don't see only the good in you."

"But you do in Billy?"

"Billy's had a hard time of it."

"Haven't we all? Look, I find it hard to work up any sympathy for a man who's been nothing but a taker all his life."

"You don't know him."

"And you do?"

"Yes. You've never seen the gentle side of him that can be tender and forgiving."

"Oh Jee—! Wake up, Emily Kate! He's never been anything but greedy. He wants, he wants, he wants — and he takes what he wants — with or without permission!"

A couple of the diners glanced our way, and I modified my tone.

"Billy can blame it as much as he wants on his neglected

childhood. But you and I — we know the difference. We were there, too."

We had been eye-to-eye across the table. Now she leaned back in her chair, forcing herself to relax.

"Different people turn out differently."

"I hope so. I'd hate to have turned out like Billy."

If I didn't know her better, I'd swear she sneered. "Oh, aren't we holier-than-thou? Do you think you're much different?"

"I hope so," I said again.

"Let's look at that. Suppose — just suppose — someone in a position of some authority were to suggest, even now, that you were involved in old man Hogan's murder. Don't you think there'd be those who'd believe it?"

"I had nothing to do with that — and you know it!" I countered.

"I know the police cleared you. But...suppose someone were to plant that seed of doubt; it's all it takes for people to start wondering."

As if I didn't know that already. Did she know something? No, there was no way she could.

"You were always around with Hanlan and Noonan in those days. Where were you the night of the murder?"

"Home in bed like I told the cops at the time."

"Yes, and your witness, Mrs. Dunn — who'd say anything you asked her to — swore to it. She's conveniently dead now, isn't she? So what if someone — anyone — were to raise questions, sow seeds of suspicion about that night. Do you think any of that might rub off on you?"

My stomach flip-flopped. How could she possibly know? She couldn't, I told myself. There was no way. So — back to bravado.

"Are you threatening me, Emily Kate?"

"Did I say that? I didn't say that. No, I'm not threatening

you. I'm just trying to show you how a story could start, how unneeded damage could be done."

"You *are* threatening me."

"Can't you see the parallel with what you're doing to Billy?"

"There is no parallel! That's pure conjecture about me. I have facts, witnesses, affidavits, the whole ball of wax against Billy. He's a crook, Emily Kate, and you'd better face it."

Her face worked as she held back the tears. "He's not a crook! He's not! How can you do this? He's my husband, the father of my—!" She looked at me, stricken. Again, I felt my stomach flip.

"You're pregnant?"

She shook her head. "I didn't mean—. There's no way—. Oh, my God, what can I do?"

She lowered her head, and a single sob escaped. I went around the table and put my arm around her shoulder.

"Take it easy, Emily Kate. I didn't know—"

Her head snapped up, eyes flashing through the tears running down her cheeks.

"You didn't know! What difference does it make? You'll keep at Billy until you destroy him. Don't you see what you're doing? You may destroy him, but in the process, you'll destroy yourself. Billy may be a bully, he may be greedy, but you're no better. You want, you want, you want, too. And you'll do anything to get what you want."

"No," I said. "No, it's different. I—"

"It's no different," she said, a tinge of despair in her voice. "There's no difference at all."

She picked up her bag.

"Wait, Emily Kate, wait a min—"

"Do what you want," she said, looking at me, the tears still in her eyes. "You'll do it anyway!"

Then she wheeled and was gone, and for a fleeting moment I knew the despair and lack of hope I'd felt those long years ago as a kid hanging from the girders of this same hotel in the seconds before Frankie Hanlan saved me. This time there was no one to save me but myself, and so far I'd made quite a hash of self-rescue.

That night, as I tossed down the doubles, I came to that moment of madness and euphoria where all my knowledge, all my talents, seemed unappreciated, and I realized suddenly that I was a genius, and that I would easily figure out how to nail Billy and how to win back Emily Kate. How could I not have seen it, it was all so clear. I would settle it tomorrow.

But by the time tomorrow arrived, everything had evaporated, and I was again what I was: a frail, uncertain, ridiculous figure with a monumental hangover.

CHAPTER 19

I was drinking too much. I knew it, but I didn't dare speak the words aloud. In my old sportswriting days, when I travelled with the teams, there were always a few cases of brew, a couple of bottles. It was part of the sports culture of the time. There were always parties and dances after victory or defeat, and I settled right into the environment, celebrating or commiserating as the case may be, often going from one to the other on the same night.

I enjoyed writing about athletes, and I often talked to them over a beer. Generally, they were people who were willing to let their actions speak for them. That never changed at the regional level, but in the majors, when the big bucks came along, athletes began to take themselves and their thoughts seriously. That marked the beginning of the end of my enchantment with sports. The death of the bigs, I wrote, agreeing with author Richard Ford, is not likely to be an assassination from ambush: it will be a slow extinction, forced by deserting fans suffering from apathy and indifference, combined with fan rage at prima donna millionaire athletes.

I had been happy to move on to straight news reporting and eventually a weekly column, although to this day some of my best friends and drinking buddies are survivors from my old sportswriting days.

Drinking, it seemed, went with every occasion. Whether it was moonshine or homebrew or Black Horse ale or Black Diamond rum, or White Star or Bacardi, or rye or lemon gin or vodka — none of it was foreign, and all of it was welcome. "There is no bad booze," we used to say, "only some that's better than others."

Shortly after my lunch with Emily Kate, I went on a

bender that lasted a week. I was able to get by the daily stories I was assigned, and I pulled out a couple of columns I'd written for emergencies such as sickness. I thought drunkenness qualified.

When I say the bender lasted a week, I don't mean it was unprincipled drinking. No, it was very well organized. I had a couple of vodkas to get my day started (usually after throwing up my first attempt), followed by a breakfast of coffee, bread, and cheese. At about 10, I'd slip out for a bracer, then a couple more at noon and maybe a sandwich and beer. Then back for a slog through the afternoon. Since the *Patriot* went to bed around noon, this was mainly a matter of preparing stories for tomorrow, checking facts, working on a column. I was usually gone by four to a favourite watering hole to spend the night.

This time I knew what was making me drink. I was hung up on what to do with the information I had about Billy Williams. On the one hand, I wanted to nail him, but on the other I didn't want to hurt Emily Kate. And the more I drank, the less I had to worry about making that decision.

The week's drinking stretched into ten days, then two weeks. Friends at the paper spoke to me in a roundabout way. The managing editor, Colin Large, suggested I take a few days off since I was "working too hard," but of course I didn't, and I got sloppier and sloppier around the office.

It was only a matter of time before I got canned, so, in a moment of alcoholic brilliance that I later regretted, I signed myself into Falconwood Hospital, the insane asylum, at that time the only place for the treatment of alcoholism. I belonged there, there was no question of that, but I doubted it would help me.

I have no recollection of my entry interview, but they told me later that I spoke about — and to — Emily Kate almost incessantly. They gave me something to knock me out and dumped me into a padded cell, but the faces that haunted my drugged state did not include Emily Kate, only those of the two men I had killed.

*

I have fleeting memories from the early days I spent in Falconwood: bars on the windows; the one they called The Rifleman chained to the radiator; the shrink remarking, "Another day, another dollar"; the yellows and reds of fall fading into the white of winter, a huge blank block of time; background information and conversation provided by the shrink and his tape recorder; strange dislocations and emotional riot. Vengeance, ingratitude, cruelty, misfortune, intrigue, revolt, ambition, remorse, enmity, madness.

I willingly volunteered for LSD experiments during which I discovered that I wore my emotions on my sleeve. I would laugh or cry at a question or a simple statement or a piece of music. I smoked a whole pack of Players, one after the other, talking furiously to the shrink, picturing the life of a farmer as the ideal I was seeking, ignoring the irony.

A farmer, I said, was what I should be, away from the pressures of the life I was leading. I learned that poorly understood and badly monitored emotions were a major problem not only for me, but interfered with every aspect of the intimate and public lives of people everywhere.

Once, with the LSD churning inside me, I turned into a fox when the attendant left me alone in the washroom, admiring my lupine features in the mirror, tongue lolling, drooling.

I took all the psychological, self-evaluation, and intelligence tests — lasting two full days that seemed a week. The only part I enjoyed, since it impressed the psychologist, was my ability to repeat seven-digit numbers, then casually rhyme them off backwards.

I often enjoyed my lack of responsibility, my surrender

of control. My drinking had been a gradual thing, insidious, nibbling away at my brain until, like a car with bald tires, I was careening on the wet pavement of my mind, out of control. At times it seemed liberating, this letting go, and in these moments I recognized that I did not have to run the world.

There were other times when I knew I could fade into the furniture, become invisible. I had developed a procedure for entering my cubicle: I stood in front of it at attention, my eyes closed, taking five deep breaths as the music swelled. Today it was Mozart's *Figaro*, with Cherubino and his charming *voi che sapete*.

I took two paces forward, eyes still closed, then one pace to the left, placing my back to the wall inside my cell. I nodded to the attendant to close the door, then I was alone in the darkness. I slid down along the smooth, thick padding, until I was squatting on my heels. I stayed there, comfortable, until the aria drifted away into haunting notes. Then I began to assimilate the room.

The puffy narrow walls pressed in on me. In the blackness I could feel them cramping. When I stood in the middle of my cell, arms outstretched, I could almost touch both walls. When I lay on the floor (which I often did since it felt cleaner than the goaty mattress) and placed my head to the door, my reaching toes came to within eighteen inches of the end of the room. The diminutive window, never open, gave little light, protected by years of grime, its postage-stamp glass made gloomier still by the crisscrossed bars. The image of the raven, wet and sleek in the rain, came into my mind each time I gazed at the window — the raven perched outside, pecking at the glass, seeking a way in through the narrow slot, the gunport in the castle — and suddenly my mind skyrocketed into Gothic images, dark, gloomy, foreboding creatures — evil. I reached out to touch one of them, understanding their torment, when my hand bumped against the bunk. I recoiled, then the image of a butcher's knife appeared before me like Macbeth's dagger, and I grabbed for it with both hands.

When my screams finally attracted the attendants, I was on my knees, struggling to destroy my bunk, through-bolted to the floor. I already had one end loose when they fell on me.

✲

Alcoholism, the shrink said, shows no favourites. It was small consolation.

CHAPTER 20

The psychiatrist said, "You'll be able to go home soon."

I said, "I love Seth McGuire. He's a grand man."

The doctor looked at me curiously. "Yes," he said. "I suppose he is."

"D'you know Seth? Isn't he a grand man?"

"Just grand. Great altogether."

"I never knew he had such depth to him. Did you?"

"Oh, I don't know him at all well."

"He can talk art and opera. Did you know that?"

"Well no, I didn't. Anyway, we're not talking about Seth McGuire."

"Well yes, we are."

He smiled. "I guess we are at that."

"Have you seen him lately?"

"Not for some time."

"How long?"

"Oh, about a year."

"A year?"

"About that."

"You don't know him at all."

"Why do you say that?"

"Seth has been dead for three years."

He pulled on his pipe, making notes.

"Tell you the truth, I never heard of him," he said.

"There you are. False pretenses. And you want *me* to be truthful."

"Sorry about that."

"Yeah."

After six weeks I was allowed home, and, after a further week, I returned to work. From the first day back, I was accepted openly and enjoyed many a laugh with my colleagues about my crazy spell. I heard often the old chestnut, "You don't have to be crazy to work here, but it sure helps. Ask Mickey."

As I returned to normal — whatever that was — I found that all my waking thoughts were of Emily Kate. I had to force her out of my mind to do my work. The shrink had told me not to call her, that the time would come for that, and that I must first try to get my life in order on my own with help from AA. This was the real world for me, but all I knew for sure was that if loneliness comprised the real world, then I was indeed back. I started to call her a dozen times but always hung up before the phone rang or after the first ring. Once I waited to hear her say "Hello," then hung up.

My determination to see her grew gradually. One day I decided that I'd call and talk to her, and simply making that decision was enough to sustain me for a week. Next, I had to consider when I'd call. I decided on next week, giving myself lots of time to prepare myself. Before the week was up, however, I'd lived through every possible scenario a dozen times until the anticipation became too much, and after three days I picked up the phone.

"Hello."

"Emily Kate, it's Mickey."

There was a long pause. "Are you supposed to be talking to me?" she said finally, and I knew the shrink had been in touch with her. A good sign or a bad sign, who could tell?

"Not if you don't want me to," I said.

"Well...it's just that the doctor said—"

"Never mind the doctor. This is you and me. Are you coming to the Island soon? Can we meet? Have a few words? I'm okay now."

It all came out in a rush. I was like a lovesick kid.

"Well, a few words, I guess, is okay. I'm coming over on Friday."

"I'll see you then." I hung up before she could change her mind.

How can I describe that meeting? She seemed slimmer, more mature, more beautiful, than when I'd seen her only a few months ago.

We were cautious with each other, careful, but as I breathed in the scent of her, I longed to take her in my arms.

"You look...better," she said tentatively.

"I feel fine. I'm on the mend."

"The doctor said—"

"Should you have been talking to the doctor about me?"

A little of the softness left her eyes. Good God, I thought, am I going to shoot myself in the foot again?

"*He* talked to *me*," she corrected. "Yes — about you."

"Sorry." I tried a smile. "And?"

"He said you'd made progress."

"I have, I think."

"And that now it was up to you."

"He's finished with me? He didn't tell me that."

"No, no, but maintenance only, I think he called it."

"Like an old car."

"Something like that, I guess."

We strolled in silence. There are three kinds of silence: the kind where the air is full of hidden daggers, a cloud bank of tension oozing its poison into the atmosphere; the kind where there is communication without words; and the kind where a question mark hangs over everything, a sense of doubt. This was the third kind. I knew I'd have to break it eventually, and I searched to find the correct words.

"I'm trying to change," I said at last.

She nodded, saying nothing.

"There've been a lot of bad things in my life," I said.

"I know. You seem to have...adjusted."

"One learns to...adapt."

"Yes."

"My God," I said, eyeing her up and down. "I forgot. You don't look pregnant."

Her eyes fell. "Miscarriage."

"Oh, Emily Kate, I'm so sorry. You would be a wonderful mother."

"Maybe."

"You would. Will you try again?"

"No. Billy—" She paused, then continued. "I want you to hear this from me. I'm leaving Billy."

My heart leapt, but hypocrite that I am, I kept it out of my face and voice.

"That's terrible, Emily Kate. I'm sorry to hear it."

"I failed him," she said.

"Why do you think it's your fault? Billy's a—"

"You were right. The stories about him are true."

I lowered my head so she wouldn't see the triumph in my eyes. I let the silence drag, the old interviewer's trick.

"How come you didn't do your story on him?"

"Didn't want to hurt you," I said. "How'd you find out?"

"I can tell when Billy's lying," she said. "You were right about something else, too — marrying Billy was the biggest mistake of my life."

It was music to my ears, but I kept my head down. You cannot even appear to gloat when a person is dealing with pain like this and what she considers personal failure.

"What can I say, Emily Kate?"

"Don't say anything. I had to tell you so you won't be surprised. It'll be quiet. I'm away all week as it is. I just won't be coming home on weekends anymore."

"Can I—?"

"Don't say anything," she repeated. "I'm happy that you're feeling better and are back to work. I'm going now. I'll call you in a few weeks."

And she was gone.

CHAPTER 21

"**P**ower," the shrink said. "The primitive quality of the schizophrenic experience demonstrates how power works." And he explained how some people, unable to cope with the frightening fragments, split off from the self, act out sometimes gruesome tyrannies over others.

"Am I schizophrenic?"

"No, but you have some of the traits."

"So, you're saying this makes me seek power over others?"

"All that — and your lousy temper."

The man was not without humour.

"Would I be likely to hit someone?"

"Of course. It wouldn't only be your biochemistry acting, but a wounded psychological self."

"I'll keep working on it."

He nodded. "Do that."

"So are you saying I'm not psychotic, doc?"

"Oh, I'd hardly go that far."

Do you wonder that I liked this man? I had not, however, told him of either of the murders, nor did I intend to.

"But," he said, "I think we can drop schizophrenia from your list of troubles."

"Oh? How come?"

"Well, you have displayed some of the symptoms — hallucinations, delusions, thought disorder, depression, social withdrawal—"

"Good God, I sound like a basket case."

"You very nearly were. But the LSD would probably have contributed. We're still experimenting with it. Most of these symptoms went away as you sobered up. I think you just had a bad case of the DTs."

"Thank God for small mercies — I guess."

"You are a bit eccentric, though."

"You're not the first one to tell me that."

"Oh, you have mental problems — we all do. But let me ask you — have you had any of these symptoms the last couple of weeks? Any at all?"

I thought a bit. "No — nothing." There was discovery and amazement in my voice.

"I think you may have bouts of depression — aggravated by alcohol — but apart from that, I think you're probably okay."

"Warped a little?"

"A little, yes."

"Depressed?"

"Some of the time. Ups and downs at times — I'd say that's average."

"No more hallucinations?"

"You should be okay if you lay off the juice."

"You're hedging, doc."

"It's what we do. Who can ever be sure?"

"It's good news, though...isn't it?"

"I'd say so. Get into the AA program. Give it a try."

"I'll do that."

✳

I tried it out in front of a mirror. "My name is Michael and I'm an — uh — a — a — problem drinker." I couldn't say it, even standing there all alone. It wasn't going to work, the doctor'd said, if I didn't accept it myself. Banjaxed with drink, I was like Stood-Up O'Brien's old dog — I'd go a step of the road with any man, admit to anything. But sober, no. Then, lies, deceit, and denial were my forte.

I threw myself into my work. We were in the midst of Premier Alex Campbell's Liberal years and the Development

Plan was upon us with its eighty-plus programs and its $725 million, all aimed at improving the overall life of Islanders.

I felt it was far-reaching and visionary and, as it progressed, it began to give Islanders a new sense of their own identity. I wrote much about the Plan, both laudatory and critical, but my overall summation was that a group inferiority complex, formed over a couple of hundred years since absentee landlords first drew lots for this old island, could not be erased overnight, but that with this guidance, Islanders could begin to believe that they would become masters of their own fate, captains of their own souls.

In those days, what I often asked myself was whether my decision to pursue a life in the newspaper business was not the search for power I'd thought it was, but the result of a poverty of soul, resulting in aridity, desiccation, cynicism, and something akin to despair. As I preached the gospel of accuracy and truth to the neophytes — the who, what, where, when, and why — I cuddled wantonly within myself my hard-won ability to camouflage and dissemble.

I tried my hand at fiction and sold several stories to some of the little magazines. I felt that at the core of the desire to create fiction is a struggle to find order in an uncertain world, the writer's attempt to impose order on the only life he knows — his own.

I felt I was creating false autobiography, false history, tearing all manner of weird and frightening grotesques from the attic of my mind. But, I insisted, this is not an imaginary life, this *is* my life. I was completely preoccupied by the first person singular, the foundation for the temple I was erecting.

Several weeks had passed and Emily Kate still had not phoned. On the spur of the moment, I decided to call on Billy Williams. I knew if I threatened him he'd get in touch with Emily Kate, and she might call me. I knew I could give him a jolt, but I doubted that I'd gain anything further from him. Anything Billy'd have to say to me at this point would be largely self-serving or unprintable.

I found him in a downcast state, unusual for Billy. With me, he always showed the smiling face, the best foot forward. When I told him I was about ready to run the story, I expected an explosion. Instead, he looked at me listlessly, raising a hand and dropping it in a "who cares?" gesture.

"This could ruin you," I said.

He shook his head and forced life into his eyes. He looked strange. "Are you on something, Billy?"

"Nothing — well, some mild tranquillizers."

"What's wrong?"

"You bastard — you have the nerve to ask me that?"

At least a sign of some fight. Then it struck me. Emily Kate's told him she's leaving him.

He shook himself. "Look," he said, "this story of yours...?"

"Yeah?"

"I really don't care about myself, but Emily Kate — don't do this to her."

Well, well, so there was some decency under that bull hide. Or was this just Billy being Billy, trying to deflect the trouble? I thought I'd try him.

"Can't wait, Billy. The story's written and ready to go."

"It'll hurt her terribly."

"Do you think so? Does it really matter anymore?"

He studied me closely, and I reminded myself that Billy couldn't have gotten where he was without strong intuition and a good feel for people.

After a few moments he nodded his head, a look of certainty on his face. "You know," he said. "About us."

"I know."

"I should have known she'd tell you."

I said nothing.

"Listen," he said, "there may be a way to spare her this—this..."

"Dirt?"

"Okay. Dirt."

I was surprised at Billy's show of nobility, but suspicious. "How?"

"Will you wait just a few days? Will you do that?"

"Why?"

"I'm not sure, but I think I can promise you an even bigger story. Well," he hedged, "at least some people might think it's bigger."

"What's bigger than a public scandal?"

I was enjoying myself. Again, the feeling of power. But there is a point beyond which it is unwise to push a person, no matter how guilty he is.

Billy's eyes hardened and the old steel was back in his voice.

"Listen, you bastard. The only reason you're not flat on your ass with a broken jaw is that I'm trying to be reasonable here for the sake of Emily Kate. If you're not interested in that then get to hell out of here before I kill you!"

"Okay. Okay. How long are we talking here?"

"A few days. Monday at the latest."

"And this is to protect Emily Kate?"

"That's right. I wouldn't lie to you about anything as important as this."

Yeah, sure. Still, something about him convinced me.

"Okay. Till Monday."

I hoped I wasn't being suckered again. I couldn't think of any way he could get out from under this time. I felt the power of an executioner granting his victim a few days of grace. This time I had him for sure.

But Billy had the last laugh as I was soon, sadly, to learn.

CHAPTER 22

Saturday's *Guardian* gave the story front page billing: "Prominent businessman and city councillor...killed in accident ...car plowed into a parked cement mixer on the side of the narrow airport road...night dark...visibility poor...."

No question that it was an accident, no sign of alcohol in the car, although I learned later there was plenty in Billy. There was no note, nothing irregular. An accident, pure and simple.

I knew it was suicide, but what could I say? Nothing. The cunning Billy had outsmarted me. Of course, he'd had to kill himself to do it. When I looked at it objectively, I thanked him. Now there were no obstacles between me and Emily Kate. But I had to proceed with care. This would take time.

It had come as a shock when the paper called Friday night. Vance Bradley, the night man, knew we had a relationship, and that I would want to know.

"I can't believe it," I said.

"A tough way to go." I could hear Vance sucking on his old pipe. "You want to do the obit, Mickey?"

"No — no, let one of the kids do it. Where's the body?"

He told me, and I called the funeral home, but they'd already called Emily Kate, and she was on her way home from Halifax.

Now, I stood with her in the cemetery with several nuns nearby and a few of her friends from the telephone company, Jack Brady among them.

"I still can't get my mind around this," I said. "I was talking to Billy only last Wednesday."

"Oh?" she said. "What about?"

"Oh, I — uh — he asked me to, you know, hold off on the story for a few days — and I, uh, agreed."

"You lie terribly — for one so used to it."

"It's no lie. I said I'd hold back on it."

"Well, you can run it now," she said bitterly.

"No, I have no wish to blacken Billy's name."

Overhead a Dart-Herald was coming in for a landing at the nearby airport. We paused until the noise dwindled.

"I'm really sorry, Emily Kate," I said.

"Are you?" she said. "Are you *really*?" She paused, as if replaying what I'd said earlier. "What do you mean, he asked you to hold off a few days?"

I knew I'd said too much. Improvise, improvise! Act, act!

"Billy was getting me more information about who the real crooks were."

"You mean he was innocent?"

"No — but there were others involved more deeply than him. Stuff like that. I'll keep digging."

"I'm sure you will. No foul play suspected?"

"No, nothing like that."

"You don't suppose...suicide...?"

"Billy? Don't be crazy, Emily Kate. He loved life too much, you know that. It was an accident."

She nodded, apparently satisfied. We were standing a little apart from the others, as if they suspected matters of importance were being discussed between us. A lone tear glistened on her cheek.

"He's at peace now," she said. "Neither of us can hurt him anymore."

"You never hurt him, Emily Kate."

"I hurt him most of all. I left him."

"It was no more than he deserved."

She drew herself up, eyes flashing. The shrink had said

that all relationships are about power, and that there are moments in a conversation when power passes from one opponent to another. This was such a moment.

"And what do you deserve, Mickey? What will you suffer? What will be your punishment?"

She turned and strode back to her friends. I noticed that the headstone where I'd been idly picking at the lichen was almost bare, a small heap gathered near my feet. The exultation that had been rising within me died.

CHAPTER 23

My association with AA, never solid, lagged. I began slipping away early from meetings, then missing them completely, then "slipping" in the AA sense of the word — drinking — at first furtively, then, when I felt it no longer mattered, publicly. Who the hell was I keeping sober for anyway? Three years and I hadn't even absorbed the leading AA principle that one had first of all to keep sober for oneself.

I decided to become a social drinker, but that phase didn't last. Staying sober, I determined, had been a good experiment, valuable in its own right, revealing traits of character, like remorse, that I thought I'd pretty well put behind me. I was somewhat amazed — and chagrined as well — that tenderness had not been completely drained from me, and I decided that this as much as anything was responsible for the self-pity I'd experienced. My soul craved the chaotic, riotous life induced by alcohol. I was so far gone in my thinking that in concurring with Oscar Wilde that "experience is the name everyone gives to his mistakes," I convinced myself that my sobriety had been a mistake, that my work required alcohol as fuel.

I abandoned self-pity, determined to take my blows like a man. Pity, I decided, was a highly overrated virtue — if, indeed, it was a virtue at all — the most evanescent force on earth, evaporating even as you used it, mostly wasted in any event. Nobody wanted pity, and the most hated of all was self-pity.

It was easy to be noble when no true test faced me. I dreamed of how I would handle danger, and hoped I would not be a coward. I invented situations for myself and imagined my reactions, brave if not heroic, trying to keep within the bounds of reality, without Superman or Batman to the rescue. I imagined my death under trying circumstances, even drowning (which I feared most), and decided that it would not be too difficult to die during some kind of activity, since one would be too intent struggling for survival to be afraid. It was the thought of dying in inaction that was terrifying — the impassive waiting, the time for thoughts of horror, the cowardly whining. No, I decided, the trick was to die at the right moment.

There is a certain kind of writer who finds his motivation in discontent and disaster, so that his art becomes a kind of crying for Elysium, seeking the ideal, trying to save the world. I strove to avoid that since I believed that one doesn't write to save the world, which one can't anyway: one writes to save oneself. And I took to heart Graham Greene's reflection that writing is a kind of therapy. "I wonder," he wrote, "how all those who do not write, compose, or paint can manage to escape the madness, the melancholia, the fear which is inherent in the human condition," and I pondered the tortured life of Greene, subject as he was, even with all the writing he did, to savage bouts of depression and despair and the melancholy he dreaded, seeking release in alcohol, drugs, travel, and sex. Well, I concluded in grim humour, we don't all have the opportunities or the wherewithal to follow in Greene's footsteps, but two out of four ain't bad.

I wrote of the value of neighbourhoods, even in a city as small as Charlottetown, as providers of sociological and psychological comfort, and an identity that comes from shared experiences and values. I did not mention the reservoirs of bitter memories, frustrated dreams, strangled expectations, and frozen economic and social mobility that resulted in paranoia and hate.

✳

The managing editor urged me to slow down, but I had

little else to keep me busy. I could get by on five hours' sleep, my mind churning incessantly. There were times when I awoke with sentences and phrases at hand, and all I had to do was jot them down, and that made me half-believe that I hadn't really slept at all. Through the night I kept a bottle handy to force down the demons.

Why did I need to drink? I don't know. I read with interest that hypertonic sodium chloride solutions when injected into the hypothalamus of goats induced them to drink large volumes of water. This was in a search for neural mechanisms controlling drinking, and I thought this held some promise, until I read further that the goats were non-selective about what they drank, and readily knocked back a mixture of urine and water indicating, the report said, "that the urge to drink was very strong."

Well, hell, I knew that already and had no desire to try the injection myself for fear of the distasteful results.

I read B. F. Skinner on how needs and wants are likely to be thought of as psychic or mental, while hungers are more readily seen as physiological; and that when a man says, for instance, "I need a taxi," he does not need a taxi in the sense of not having had a taxi for a long time. If we wish to induce a man to hail a taxi, I read, we put him in a position to require a taxi, we do not deprive him of taxis.

As the boys in the West End used to say, "This is common dog turd," meaning that this is the sort of wisdom known instinctively by any moron.

It seemed best to stop tinkering with my mind, to try to get back to the idea of one day at a time or even one hour at a time, to get out and about more, to seek someone to share my life with.

Since I had not heard from Emily Kate as she'd promised, I decided on the spur of the moment to call, and dialled her number before I had a chance to consider the wisdom of the act. She asked me if I had any particular reason for calling.

"Just to hear your voice," I said. I added into the pause that followed before it became embarrassing, "I was just wondering how you were getting along."

"I'm doing fine."

"I'm pleased to hear it."

"My faith has been a great comfort to me."

I stayed silent.

"I know you have no use for the Church," she said, "but it's been good for me."

"Damn superstition."

There was a pause, giving me time to regret ever phoning.

"Did you call me to abuse me?"

"No, no, I didn't. It's just—"

"Don't you ever question my faith. Question your own if you like, but don't attack mine. And if you can't stay off matters that are important to me, perhaps you shouldn't call me at all."

There was a gentle click as she hung up.

❊

Oh, the times weren't all bad. There were moments I felt the joy of living, a surge of happiness. But as soon as I did, guilt began to intervene, bringing me back to the horrors of my existence. I had nothing or nobody else to blame at this point, so I blamed the Church for keeping Emily Kate from me, for inflicting me with such a monumental sense of guilt, never admitting that I had plenty to be guilty about.

❊

God is just, we are told, just but tough. Well, if you study the Bible, you can only conclude that God is a flawed character, maturing as he ages, true, but certainly — you should excuse it — no saint. He is a man of many personalities.

Just after the great act of creation, for instance, when he

nabs Adam and Eve, he acts not charitably nor forgivingly, but vindictively, driving them out of the Garden of Eden. Then, later, he gets really pissed off and sends the flood over the earth, wiping out all but Noah and his clan and the family pets. No simple hurricane for God. No, sir, total immersion or nothing. Take no prisoners.

In his developing and conflicted personality, in the Book of Isaiah, God mixes the roles of executioner with visionary. But in the Book of Job, his full destructive impulse explodes on poor unsuspecting and innocent Job, only to be followed, to God's credit, by remorse and repentance.

All I can conclude is that if contradictory behaviour is good enough for God, who am I to complain?

Like most men, I want something greater than myself. Is there a middle ground where I can believe, but only a little? The prayer of the lustful sinner springs to mind: "Lord, make me good, but not just yet." If one has to go wholeheartedly to God, then forget it, I can't do it. Thoughts of the damnation of the lukewarm haunt me. Someone wrote arguing for a modest, tentative, and skeptical acceptance of the world. It's what I try to do: *que sera, sera*. But it seldom works.

CHAPTER 24

I played the tape the doctor had given me.

"...mind being alone?"

"Why should I mind? I enjoy it," I heard myself saying.

"It's not the usual state. The pantry of self must be well-stocked to handle solitude."

"The pantry of self, eh? I like that, doc."

"I read it somewhere."

"Can I use it?"

"Feel free."

"I've got enough groceries to last a while, doc."

"You're going to make me sorry I said it, aren't you?"

"Solitude no longer holds fear for me."

"But it did?"

"Once upon a time — long ago."

"So now you're over it — you can handle it?"

"Most of the time, most of the time."

"How?"

"Well...it requires a certain discipline. It's like single-handed sailing. If anything goes wrong, if anything has to be done, *you* have to do it because there's no one there but you."

"You like single-handed sailing?"

"I do."

"Why?"

"Who knows? No phone, no silly chattering. Alone with the sea, the sky, the elements. It's basic stuff. You feel brave — man against the indifferent sea — if only out as far as Fitzroy Rock."

"No fear?"

"Oh yes — especially if it blows up. Aren't you afraid of the sea? Of drowning? But that's part of it — the challenge."

"You have to prove yourself?"

"You don't have to, but it gives an edge to your life."

"You need that?"

"Look, doc, my life has been shaped by solitude — the place where I hide and reflect, and as someone said, 'wait for the eternal silence.' So, yes, I need a challenge. It's part of my pantry's stock."

※

Why had the shrink given me that tape? All he'd said was to play it, listen to it. It didn't take a genius to realize the doctor was pointing out my isolation as self-imposed, but was he also saying that it wasn't good, wasn't necessary? Was he suggesting gregariousness? Forget it.

I decided to make a tape of my own and give it to the doctor. Of my time alone, like *Krapp's Last Tape*. The shrink knew Beckett; we'd talked about the humour and the hope in *Godot*.

On bad days, my dreams were confused and broken. I studied the great writers, read of their lives, and concluded that genius and disease and madness and sanity, were, like strength and mutilation, somehow tied up together. I felt I was becoming fussy and a stickler for detail. I read Fowler just for enjoyment. I even accepted the snorting remarks of my colleagues at the newspaper: "There is no God but Fowler, and Casey is his prophet."

I recalled the dictum: "Times change; people don't," and concluded that the belief that human behaviour and aspirations are constants, even if contexts change, was another principle foisted on the public as a defence for poor behaviour and an unwillingness to change. People *do* change; the past *is* a foreign country, and they do, indeed, do things differently there.

※

"Can you face the fact that you can't have Emily Kate?"

"I can't do that, doc."

"Can you learn to live without her?"

"No."

"You're doing okay."

"I'm not."

"Tell me about it."

"It's only more of the same."

"Tell me anyway."

"How close do you think the end of the world is?"

"What!?"

✳

Okay, now I'm taping this session just for you, doc. Just a minute. Ahhhhh, that's better. Where was I? Solitude. Not all solitary people are unhappy; many people may not have raised families or formed close personal ties, but surely not all of them have been unhappy. Look at some of the great loners — and, ha, ha — I'm not comparing myself to them, doc, just pointing out that if they can live solitary, relatively happy lives, even if some of them were noted as being a touch odd — perhaps a trait of aloneness — then ordinary mortals can do the same.

Pascal, Kant, Newton, Kirkegaard, Descartes, Nietzsche, Spinoza, Locke, Leibniz, Schopenhauer, Wittgenstein. None married; most lived alone most of their lives. One thing — they didn't have wives pissed off at them if they took a drink now and then. Which reminds me...ah, yes....

Let's continue.... Solitude — the great leveller. A man who can stand his own company for long periods of time can survive anything. Naturally, there are hallush— hallush— hallushinations. Read any account of single-handed sailing: how the talking begins, how you populate the cockpit, even chat with the birds that land in the rigging. Takes an iron will, courage. Look at poor Donald Crowhurst. Went starkers somewhere in the South Atlantic after running two sets of logs, faking his position reports, claiming conquest of the Roaring Forties and the Horn, yet never got farther south than the Falklands, left his false records intact, finally jumped overboard. Didn't have the strength up here. Let the record show, your honour, that the witness tapped his head at this point in his testimony.

Or what about those old monks, chased out of a warm bed at midnight, at two, four, six, into a freezing chapel, fasting, deprived of sleep, repeating the same chant over and over, becoming disoriented and giddy. Is it any wonder they hallushinated? Or like St. Kevin, all alone and freezing his arse off in his little stone cell in the hills of Glendalough, he'd be damn glad of a vision or two to keep him company, wouldn't he?

I tell you, doc, I can see the ads of the day calling for young men to come and study and pray in the lonely monasteries: "Visions guaranteed or your worldly goods cheerfully refunded."

Solitude. Relationships get less important as we get older, a gift perhaps from a kinder nature. Why? To ease the inevitable parting of loved ones? Hah! No problems for me there. Emily Kate? What about her? Haven't seen her for ages. Marriage? To her? Don't be crazy. If we didn't look to marriage as the principal source of happiness, fewer marriages would end in tears and recriminations. Insight — thash an insight, doc, not a big one, maybe, just an excuse, man can rationalize anything, can't he?

Ahhhhhh. Great stuff, doc. Very tasty. Where was I? Solitude? Who the hell cares? Why do so many of you professionals conshider that intimate pershsonal relationships are the chief source of happiness? Eh? Eh? That a man can't be happy alone? Eh? You forgot what Freud said — that what constitutes psycho— psycholosh— psycholoosh— screw it! — mental health, is the ability to love and to work! To work!

See? Too much emphasis on love, not enough on work. Work, see? What makes the world go round. Forget this deshpair stuff, doc, work, that's it, work and soli— sholi— sholish— Loneliness!

✳

My world has changed. The landmarks of my childhood are mostly gone now as if the city were trying to forget itself — or reinvent itself. Gone are Rix's Grocery, P.J. McCloskey's, White's Restaurant, Fennel and Chandler's, Larter's Barber Shop, the Maple Leaf Bakery, the Revere Hotel, and all the rest. Nothing remains as it was, and that's the name we give to progress. When I stand at the Fire Station corner and stare east along Kent Street and south down Queen Street and see and hear in my mind the boisterous streets of my youth, am I inventing a brighter past, am I remembering times that never were? And when my gaze slows at the former site of old Doyle's store, and my mind sinks under the weight of pain and misery and guilt, is my black sense of rage still real? Could I kill him again? Yes, probably.

The past is not a world I wish to dwell in.

✳

"Power," the doctor said. "I keep coming back to it. If I can borrow from Max Weber: power is the influence one person uses to realize his own end in a joint action, even against the resistance of another who is also participating in the action."

I absorbed this.

"Is every conversation a power struggle?" I asked.

"With you, it seems so."

"You're getting personal, doc."

"You're right."

"So what do I do?"

He inspected his nails.

"You have a tendency to get into the same mess over and

over again."

"So you've told me. Repetition compulsion."

He gave me his knowing smile and a nod.

"What do you think of this?" he said. "There's a school of thought that holds that mental disorders and personality development are primarily determined by interpersonal interaction rather than by constitutional factors."

"By relationships with others?"

"That's right. Emotional misery has its roots in experiences with others."

"Hmmmmm," I said helpfully.

"It's a theory that questions the neurobiological view and looks for sources in real life, rather than in fantasy."

"Is that a fact?"

"It goes on to suggest that the mad person is an active agent in the creation and perpetuation of his own misery, and must choose, finally, to abandon his abnormal isolation in favour of authentic relatedness to others in order to regain his sanity."

"You keep ranking me with the nuts, doc. It's doing nothing for my self-esteem."

"The first step in a self-cure is falling ill, then beginning to change."

"What are you suggesting? That I tell everyone I'm crazy? That I tell them I'm learning to love myself? That I go about declaring my love for my fellow man?"

"Now you're getting it."

CHAPTER 25

I heard that Emily Kate was back from Halifax, staying at the Charlottetown Hotel. I went there around noon and waited in the lobby.

She halted leaving the elevator when she saw me. I made my eyes glad to see her, but there was nothing in her stare, only recognition. Her beauty emphasized my shabbiness.

"I wondered how long it would take," she said.

"I came as soon as I heard."

No handshake, no touch, nothing.

"I don't think I want to see you right now."

"Welcome to you, too, Emily Kate."

"Will this take long? I have an appointment for lunch."

Her eyes had not softened. She was not going to make this easy for me.

"Still suspicious of me?"

Her eyes narrowed, but she said nothing. She pursed her lips and gave her head a little tilt to the side as if saying that she hadn't changed her mind about that. I started to object, then thought better of it. Any defensive words would only dig me into a deeper hole. I let it drop.

"How do you like Halifax?" I asked.

She shrugged. "I like it."

"Seeing anyone?"

"Don't be so crass. Anyway, that's none of your business."

"I know. But are you?"

"Are you?"

"No — and no prospects."

She sized me up, her gaze impartial, as if either measuring me for a noose or satisfying herself that she knew why my prospects were nil.

Finally, she spoke. "Same here."

How to explain it: my heart leapt, soared, took off through the roof, but I kept it from my face.

"You deserve better," I said.

"I do, don't I? But...I feel a certain sense of guilt about Billy."

"You have nothing to feel guilty about."

"But I do anyway."

"Goddam Catholic guilt!"

"Keep your filthy tongue off the Church, you— pagan!"

It was probably the worst thing she could think to call me. I shook my head, wiped my face. I had not realized it was so hot in here.

"Can we go outside?" I said. "Walk a bit?"

We walked up to the corner, then across Queen Street down towards Great George Street. We said nothing, and the silence, I thought, grew almost companionable.

"You'd better start talking soon," she said.

"I don't know where to start. I've waited for this day, considered all the things I wanted to say to you — and now my mind is blank."

"That doesn't happen to you a lot, does it?"

I smiled. "No. The business I'm in, you always have to have a question."

"Well, don't start with me. This is no interview."

"Goddam it, Emily Kate, loosen up."

"Not going the way you'd planned, is that it?"

I paused, knowing she was right. My elation soured.

"That's right," I said. "You're right, of course you're right, you're always right."

For the first time, a hint of a smile. "Why is that such a surprise?"

"Emily Kate, my guardian, my saviour, my caretaker, my

protector."

"You don't need my protection any longer," she said gently.

"I need somebody's," I said, my voice as gentle.

We walked a few moments in silence.

"It's strange," she said, "but I have this sense of, I don't know, almost betrayal."

"I haven't betray—"

"I know."

I knew all about betrayal, both the large variety and the small; I was a connoisseur of betrayal — from both sides of the coin. I played one side now.

"I've been betrayed once or twice myself, Emily Kate."

It was her turn to pause, reflect, remember.

"Sorry."

"Don't be sorry. It's me. I haven't lived a day without—"

"I must be going," she said suddenly.

I took a moment to recover. "Anyone I know?"

She smiled sardonically. "Yes — although you haven't seen them for years." She paused. "A couple of the nuns."

"From the old days?"

"Yes. They're out at the Mount. I'm seeing them there."

"Maybe we could get together later?"

"I think not. I'm flying back this evening."

"I could take you to the airport."

"No."

"Well, that's direct enough."

"Look, Mickey, I can't afford to see you, can you understand that?"

My heart bounced.

"Does that mean...?"

"Don't read anything into it."

"I just thought that maybe—?"

"Don't. Don't think anything."

It would have to be enough. For now.

"All right," I said. "Goodbye, Emily Kate."

I wanted to take her in my arms, console her, assure her that I was a different person now, but of course I wasn't, so I did nothing. She turned and started down the street towards Ed's Taxi. The last I saw of her was a flash of stocking as she climbed into Lenny Arsenault's cab. Lenny smiled and waved as he closed the door, and I waved back automatically, thinking that I would probably never see her again.

The accumulative punishment for all my crimes gathered in one monumental pool of misery and self-doubt, and, instead of any solution to my battered life, I found myself less complete, more fearful, with a personality on the verge of dissipation and disintegration.

Gide had it right: humility opens the gates of heaven; humiliation opens the gates of hell.

✻

Stomach pains, at times crippling, kept me awake at night. The brandy and whiskey and cigarettes took a licking at these times. The shrink referred me — probably an ulcer.

The specialist said, "Sit down."

"That bad?"

"Not good."

"Not an ulcer?"

"Not an ulcer."

We sat and stared at each other.

"Well?"

"I have only one thing to tell you. Ease off on the drinking or you'll be dead."

"That is bad news."

"I know it shocks you to hear it."

"Ease off — not quit?"

"Quitting would be better, but I know you, Mickey. Your system wouldn't stand complete abstinence — not right away."

"I tried it once."

"I know."

"Didn't like it."

"I know that, too."

We sat there looking at each other. He said, "I were you I'd get away for a while. Try for a new perspective."

"The geographical cure. I hear it doesn't work."

"No, no, not move away. Just take a trip, think about things. Surely there's some place you'd like to visit."

"I always wanted to see Ireland."

"Well, there you are."

❊

I thought often of suicide, but, like the sins of sex, the sin of suicide was immutably planted in my heart as being the most unforgivable, and I dreaded it being my last senseless act.

That's when I started — praying may be too strong a word — but anyway hoping for impossible things, like maybe that gene therapy would become a reality, the legal infusion of genetically altered cells into a human being aimed at such human afflictions as cancer, muscular dystrophy, Alzheimer's, multiple sclerosis, depression, alcoholism. I could be built into a new man, with the end of all ailments. Hell, I could live forever. Roll on, gene therapy!

Thoughts like that gave me a proper perspective on my insignificance. And yet. And yet. As puny as our life is, we cling to it, we do not go gentle into that long, unending night. I considered the words of Irish writer Sean Hughes: "I'd like to thank God for screwing up my life and at the same time not existing, quite a remarkable skill."

❊

Despite my searching, I could not find a cure, probably because there was none, for a stony heart.

I went occasionally to Mass, especially funeral Masses, about which there was little of the old menacing sense of last things. I regretted again that the Church no longer sang the "*Dies Irae*" and the mournful final lament that always tore at my soul, "*Libera, libera me, Domine....*" For me, these were the true reminders of a final end.

I had difficulties with the Mass. Ever since the days of Good Pope John, I'd had difficulties with the Mass. Gone was the esoteric Latin and with it some of the mystery and the majesty. Gone was the stately and dignified Gregorian Chant, replaced by strumming guitars and commonplace music and lyrics that Nashville would have rejected. With all this demystification of the Mass, the Catholic Church lost something and, in my view, it was the sense of wonder that the ceremonial rites used to instill. It is all very well to simplify the Mass in an attempt to make it more accessible, but when you oversimplify it, you have removed the need of trust, of faith. It becomes just another sing-along, and not a very entertaining one at that. It is all very well to insist that the Mass itself is unchanged, but, in the eyes of people like me, brought up on its unchanging ritual, it was indeed changed, with something taken away, and it was never quite the same again.

Why could the Church not see that when you remove the mystery, you remove the need to obey? It's like God himself. If you can demystify God, understand him, if he's on the same level as yourself, just one of the boys, why bother bowing the knee? If he's not up there hurling thunderbolts, why bother hunkering down? I can hear the new catechists: "Religion is not built on fear." Well, let me tell you, Jack, it bloody well is — or it was when I was a kid, and whoever it was suggested that a child is formed in his first five or six years was right. These things don't pass with time; nothing passes with time.

And the handshakes. I'm not a fastidious person by nature, but still I can never go through the hand-to-hand combat at the invitation, "Let us offer each other a sign of peace," without wondering which of those fingers I touch have recently been scratching crotches or backsides, or fishing a wayward morsel from a decaying molar, or digging at a scrofulous head, or picking a snuffling nose. Especially during the flu-ridden days of winter, I wondered if any estimate could ever be made of the billions of germs exchanged during these handshakes. Rubber gloves should be passed out at the door.

My problem was that of the ever-changing identity of the self: Who am I? or, Who am I today? Am I the detached observer, outside myself, paring my nails, or, like Beckett's Moran, preoccupied by certain questions of a theological nature? Could I not bow the knee to some deity, or was I destined to be a recusant, to shout *"Non serviam!"* to my dying day?

When I started writing fiction, I began as a student of human inconsistency, and wrote, when I could successfully shade their identity, of people who, on the surface, lived prescribed lives, but in their own secret world engaged in sometimes bizarre and contradictory behaviour: the police officer who enforced the law as vigorously as he beat his wife; the wealthy lawyer, a pillar of the Church, at the rail weekly, on the parish council, who sought and received annulments from not one but two wives, both of whom had borne him children; or of outlawed loners like myself.

My judgement may have been too harsh, but I hated hypocrisy, my own as well as that of others. Anger blocked me. Spirituality evaded me.

✻

Without much hope, I wrote to Emily Kate, telling her I was flying to Ireland, and I'd have an hour's layover in Halifax. When she wrote back saying she'd be there to see me off, I was immediately on guard. This was too easy, and my paranoid antennae reached into the skies, searching for the source of attack.

We sparred, gently at first, then more seriously, as we sat over coffee.

"I've been thinking about Billy's death," she said.

Billy again!

"Oh, for God's sake, Emily Kate, can't you let it go," I said, feigning graciousness. "Billy's been dead, what — six years?"

"Five."

"It seems like the far distant past."

"Not to me. The past is always there — haunting me."

"I can't fight the past," I said. "I'm sick of it anyway. Why can't the past ever leave off? Why is it forever clawing at us like a wildcat?"

She shook her head. She was remarkably cool, like one who'd rehearsed all the possible lines and was prepared for anything.

"It's just that so many things...this feeling...."

The actor was standing back, evaluating, knowing risk might be necessary.

"Billy's gone this long while, Emily Kate," I said gently. "Let him rest in peace."

"He said nothing to you, when you saw him before he died?"

"No. Nothing to suggest—"

"I still find it so difficult. He was always a careful driver — even drunk."

"I know."

"He must have been doing seventy, the police said, when he hit the cement mixer."

"Right. That's what they said."

"He made no attempt to swerve, to brake — no skid

marks. It was like he aimed the car at it and went full out."

"Look," I said, putting it together for her, wording it carefully, "I've thought a lot about this, too. Billy was smart. It would not be above him to do the act — without a note or anything — knowing that you'd doubt it, knowing that you'd do just what you did — look to me as somehow guilty. That way he'd avoid the scandal, get back at me, and," I added snidely, "have the last laugh — even from the grave."

I expected an explosion, but instead she eased back in her chair, nodding, thoughtful.

"Yes," she said. "I thought of that, too."

"You did?"

"I was aware of some of Billy's...shortcomings. But there was one other reason you didn't mention."

"Oh?"

"Maybe he was thinking to spare me."

I didn't want to give Billy that much credit, although I knew from my last talk with him that that was the main reason he'd done what he'd done. Emily Kate had put her finger on it because she was aware of what she meant to Billy, and I was forced to admit it.

"You could be right," I said grudgingly. I didn't want to damn the dead except by faint praise.

"So," she said, "maybe suicide after all."

"Maybe."

"Does that mean I should return the insurance money?"

"Hardly. They're satisfied it was an accident, and you're not sure it wasn't."

There was a pause. She moved the cutlery around, then the salt and pepper, poking with her finger.

"You know....," she began.

"What?"

"No. Nothing."

"C'mon, something's bothering you. What?"

She looked at me fiercely. "I was going to say that for a guilty man you carry it well."

It was becoming a question — doesn't it always? — of who was the better actor.

"I thought we just cleared that up."

"Not Billy. I accept you weren't involved in his death. But I've been thinking again about Peter Hogan."

My stomach sank, but I smiled genially.

I figured it was about time to show her I'd had enough of her suspicions.

"Dammit to hell, Emily Kate, if you're going to accuse me, accuse me!"

She was calm, unruffled.

"How come your friends Hanlan and Noonan didn't implicate you?"

"Because I wasn't there."

"You were always hanging around with them."

"Not that night."

"Why not?"

"What is this, the third degree? I went through this with you once before. I wasn't there because it was too damn cold."

She jumped in. "So you knew their plans?"

"No. I knew they were hinting at some big score. Hell, those two were always talking about some big score."

She nodded. "You were there. I know it."

I played my ace. "Well, why didn't they say so? You knew those two — they'd have grabbed at any way out."

"Maybe not."

I was exasperated. "Why not, for God's sake?"

"It would be against Frankie's religion to squeal."

She understood Hanlan better than I did.

"That's just plain crazy when you're fighting for your life. How about Noonan? He'd talk."

"He'd do what he was told." She shifted gears. "Why did you go to see them in jail?"

"How'd you know about that?" For the first time, I was rattled.

"Tinker Martin told me — a long time ago. Said he couldn't make heads or tails of the conversation."

This came as a shock. The actor stood aside admiringly.

"There was little to make sense of. Just 'sorry for your troubles' — that sort of thing. I felt I had to say goodbye."

"I think there was more to it than that. Tinker said that Noonan was mad at you, but Hanlan kept him in check."

I shook my head. "No, there was no more to it than that. Noonan never liked me."

Risk, the actor said, take the risk. Live on the edge.

"I—" I started. I was going to tell her I was only the lookout, but I stopped in time, suddenly, acutely, aware of the disaster that would be.

She eyed me sharply. "What?"

I fought down the panic, forcing gentleness into my voice, a smile to my face.

"Nothing." I paused. "Well, I was just going to say that I felt sorry for them."

"Sometimes you surprise me," she said. "Sometimes you seem to have real feelings."

Smile! Smile! Act! Act! Live the role!

They called my flight. "That's me," I said, shoving away from the table. She rose and reached over and touched my cheek.

"When are you due back?"

I told her the flight, the date, the time.

"I'll meet you," she said. "Send me a postcard from Ireland."

I kissed her cheek, held her loosely for a moment. "I'll do that."

She turned and left, and I watched her until she was out of sight. She did not look back.

I strode down the corridor towards the departure gate, my step light, my heart trembling within me.

I've pulled it off, I thought. I've pulled it off!

The secret power of the dissembler is to be and not to be oneself, to be oneself and at the same time someone else. You are never simply one self; there is always a second self standing beside you, observing, evaluating, remembering. And I was good at it. You learn to live your role.

✳

There's an old Irish saying that when a child turns from its parents, that it is "making strange." It comes from the belief that the fairy folk sometimes steal a baby and leave a changeling in its place. It is not inconceivable, I thought, that I am indeed a changeling, and, if so, not responsible for my terrible deeds. Call it what you will — disbelief in superstition, conscience maybe, or the remnants of same, but I could not accept that explanation. As I embark on my end years, I find I am considering religious matters more and more. Is it true that there is a Hell? Is there a special place in it for those like me, guilty of violent crimes? Is it worse for those who deny their culpability?

Long after my time with the shrink, I read of the harrowing kinds of neurological damage that can come from being reared in an inhospitable world, how a bad childhood can leave people not only slow-witted but violent, how the stress of growing up under trying circumstances can cause an imbalance in serotonin and noradrenaline in the body, two neurotransmitters used to send signals to the brain.

The result can be a person constantly on high alert, seeing a disapproving word or a request for quiet as a threat demanding immediate retaliation. Life is one long emergency, the hour is always late, and the time for desperate measures is always at hand.

Could a shortage or an abundance of serotonin or nor-adrenaline be blamed for my actions? It's a handy excuse, one my mind craves to accept. But in my inner self, once again, what remains of my conscience knows this to be false.

Conscience, the nuns had taught us, is moral awareness, an inner sense in our hearts of right and wrong, and it is becoming more and more difficult for me to escape the religious views delivered by the good Sisters: It is David's "heart" that smites him when he commits acts offensive to God. It is Job's "heart" that finds him righteous. St. Paul said that the Gentiles had the law "written in their hearts," and that their conscience bore witness to it.

I can never dwell long on such matters without being filled with remorse and anxiety, finally cramming all feelings into the back of my mind, seeking solace in the nearest bottle, possibly lowering my serotonin level still further and kicking off a cycle of irritability, depression, maybe even violence once again.

Won't God ever leave me alone? Must every step of my wayward life be a battle with Him?

CHAPTER 26

The young priest spoke to me as I was leaving the Cathedral.

"You're a visitor here?"

"I am."

"And what part of America would you be from?"

"I'm a Canadian, Father."

"Ahhh. Sorry about that."

"It's no matter. Everybody says the same thing."

He was sturdily built, about thirty, with dark curly hair, an open friendly face, eyes that did not seek to betray. He seemed my idea of what a priest should be.

"So how do you like it here?"

"Great city, Galway."

"They say it's the fastest-growing city in Europe."

"So I've heard." Indeed, every bus driver, cabbie, bartender made the same boast.

He laughed and his face lit up. "I daresay you've heard little else. We like to brag about our city."

"Well, there's plenty to brag about — the theatres, the churches, the history, the pubs."

"They say we have 130 pubs in Galway. Can that be true, do you think?"

"A fair estimate, I'd say."

He pursed his lips, nodding. The exiting congregation swirled around us.

"Have you been to Connemara?"

"I have. Beautiful country up that way."

"It's my home — Letterfrack. D'ye know it?"

"I do. Near Kylemore Abbey."

"You've got it. Famine country — wild, lonely."

"I like that about it."

"You don't mind solitude and silence?"

"I'm used to being alone."

He spoke of a nearby Retreat House I might be interested in.

"Oh, I don't think so, Father."

His brows raised and lowered.

"Well, maybe not. It's a great place to think and meditate on what it's all about."

"Perhaps I'll look in on it."

"I'll show you around Saturday afternoon if you like. Come along, why don't you?"

"Why this special interest, Father?"

The Irish trick: one good question deserves another.

"Ah, there's nothing special about it. I encourage everybody to think about their life."

"The best I can do, Father, is give you a definite 'maybe.'"

"Ah sure, that's fine. It's up to you entirely."

I liked him. I'm sure he knew he was easy to like and used this to his — and the Church's — advantage. There was no way I was ever going to visit a monastery.

I'd come up from Shannon by bus, about two hours, through Ennis and Gort, and took a taxi from the station to where I was staying in Dominick Street, the Granary Suites, so-called since they had been converted from an old granary that overlooked the Corrib River. A large bay window in my self-contained unit jutted out over the water, giving a great view of the nearby William O'Brien Bridge, and to the south the Wolfe Tone Bridge, the Spanish Arch, the Claddagh, Galway Bay, and on the horizon the mountains of Clare.

I walked incessantly the first week. Like most Irish cities, Galway's centre is easily accessible by foot, and I wandered through the ancient narrow streets to Eyre Square, by the

Canal to the Cathedral, along the walk at the edge of the bay through the Claddagh to Salthill. I discovered six Catholic churches, each within a ten-minute walk of my place, and as well the historic Collegiate Church of St. Nicholas, now Church of Ireland, but once an RC church before its "conversion" by Cromwell when he destroyed Galway in 1652, and where Christopher Columbus is said to have prayed in 1477.

I discovered the theatres, and spent hours in the world-famous Kenny's Bookstore and Art Gallery in High Street, and behind it, in Middle Street, Charlie Byrne's Used and Discounted Bookshop.

I found pubs where I felt comfortable: the Galway Arms, the Lisheen, O'Connell's, O'Flaherty's, but especially Murphy's on High Street where the regulars were more men of my age, and I got to know and be known by the bartenders. Pub food was good, the Guinness better. This was a life I could adapt to.

In the Cathedral bookstore I picked up a book by Thomas Merton and read: "Our real journey in life is interior." I thought on that a good deal during several days of bus tours: to the lonely mountains of Connemara, to County Clare and the imposing Burren and the majestic Cliffs of Moher, to historic Aughrim and Athlone. It was country that encouraged meditation.

I visited the university library and spent many pleasant hours there reading and writing. It's what I'd done most of my adult life; I often had to write things out to determine what I really thought about them. As E. M. Forster once said: "How do I know what I think until I see what I say?"

In moments of depression and self-doubt, I was haunted and bedevilled by childhood ghosts of hell and damnation induced by my early Catholic teaching, fears and hatred that had finally driven me into apostasy. But I didn't hate the Catholic Church; I hated the authoritarian form it had held in my early years.

Some of the priests of those days had been rigid in their mission, allied with the forces of authority. They were narrow and intolerant, lacking charity, and yet it's the song that matters, not the singer, and I could not let religion go.

I felt full of contradictions, yet in the churches of Galway I found a quiet, a contentment, as if here I could stop the frenetic pace, get off the treadmill, come to rest. I wondered what emotions were working in me, and if what I was feeling was what drove people into churches in their old age. I thought not. I remembered I'd felt the same when I'd visited Walden Pond many years ago and sat in meditation, concluding that if as Thoreau said, he'd paid only $28 and change to erect his shack, he'd more than got his money's worth for the peace and contentment it provided. Besides, my church visits were more for a rest from walking than for prayer.

I read the poetry of Valentin Iremonger, thinking that with a name like that, how could he be anything but a poet?

It won't always be summer — not for us. There are
bad times coming,
When you and I will look with envy at old
photographs, remembering how we stood....

On a table in the vestibule of the Cathedral, I picked up a pamphlet giving details of an upcoming Novena, and on the same day read in the Galway *Advertiser* that thousands were expected to attend this "spiritual cleansing," a nine-day festival of faith. The brochure said, "If you are not a practising Catholic, God is calling you to come home and find peace."

More out of curiosity than anything else, I decided to drop in one night. The Cathedral was packed, and I had to stand at the back. The subject was Reconciliation, what we used to call Confession, but the modern Church downplays that element, emphasizing the "welcome home" to the prodigal, rather than the "God hates that sin and for your Penance say..." of the past. It was all very positive and uplifting, "feel-good psychology" at its best. That was the night I met Father Gerald Flaherty.

Saturday came, and, since I had nothing better to do, I decided to visit the monastery. I found myself in a secluded, walled area with wide lawns, flower beds, and quiet, the walls preventing all but a hissing from the traffic that crossed the nearby Salmon Weir Bridge.

"Aha! There you are," said Father Flaherty.

"I thought I'd take a look," I said non-committally.

"To be sure. No obligation, as they say in the ads. No salesman will call."

"You'd make a good salesman. You *are* a good salesman."

He smiled. "Let me show you around."

He took me into the main building, which had a smell of church to it, and into a small chapel. I was surprised to see several cowled monks praying. We knelt for a few seconds — a visit, we used to call this bit — then went out another door down a long narrow passageway with doors leading off it.

"How come the monks?" I asked.

"Cistercians — you know, Trappists. A few at a time come up here from Mount Melleray in Waterford for special Retreats. They're just finishing up today. Here, if you'd be interested in staying over, this is the kind of room you'd have."

He opened a door. A plain room about eight by ten, a single bed with a lamp over it, a desk and chair, a small table lamp, a bookcase holding several volumes, a narrow clothes closet in one corner, a washbasin in another. Spartan would be a generous way to describe it.

"No frills," he said.

"I suppose the TV's out for repairs?"

He smiled but said nothing.

"I'd have to think on it," I said eventually.

"To be sure. How long are you with us here in Galway?"

"Another ten days."

"Ah sure, a day or two here would do you no harm." He passed me a card on which he'd written his name and phone number. "Now, if you decide to come — or even if you don't and just want to chat — give me a call anytime."

We went into the kitchen where we had tea and cookies — biscuits, to the Irish.

"This place is like a little oasis," I said.

"I never come through the front gate into the garden, but a sense of peace comes over me."

"Like the descent of the Holy Ghost?"

He laughed. "Nothing so grand. Just 'God's in His heaven, All's right with the world.'"

"I felt it myself."

I was suddenly afraid. What in hell am I doing here, going on about my feelings like a bloody schoolgirl? And to a priest? This is the enemy. Subtle, crafty, insidious.

"Well, I'll be going now," I said abruptly, standing. "No — never mind — I'll find my own way out."

Three days later I called and made arrangements to come in for a day.

✻

"Much is made of the wish to be alone, of the fear of being alone, yet little is ever mentioned about the ability to be alone."

His voice was soothing with the pleasant rise and fall of the West, aided by the distant rippling of the Corrib on its way to the sea.

"The withdrawn state is usually associated with dark ideas slinking at the edge of the mind, and the sting of bitterness because of one disappointment or another. Yet through solitude we can help get rid of the false self lingering within us, a self based on compliance with others' expectations. The capacity to be alone depends on secure attachments, on being oneself without anxiety, and this is linked with self-discovery, with becoming aware of one's deepest needs, feelings, impulses, shortcomings...many feel it's a nasty journey for the little that's in it....am I going too fast?"

"Is this the crash course, Father?"

"D'ye recognize the feelings, then?"

"Some of them. But then I've always felt alone, always been alone."

"More reason to use solitude to your advantage, don't you think?"

Over time, he spoke of the insights motivated by solitude, of the great religious leaders retreating from the world to seek answers: of Buddha meditating on the banks of the Nairanjan; of Jesus spending forty days in the wilderness, returning with his message of repentance and salvation; of Mahomet withdrawing to the caves of Hera during the month of Ramadan; of the old Irish monks like St. Kevin in his cold stone cell in the hills of Glendalough — all using solitude to gain insight and bring about positive changes in their own personalities.

I explained to him my theory of hallucinations caused by such fasting and lack of sleep, and he said, "You're probably right, but no matter if they were hallucinations, visions, mystical experiences, whatever, there's no denying that they had a positive and therapeutical effect and provided emotional support for the participants."

My "one day" became two, the two became three, and by the time I blinked, a week had passed. During that time more monks arrived from Mount Melleray, and one afternoon I witnessed two of them at daggers drawn, uttering not a word, in silent combat over I knew not what, frowning, gesticulating, pounding the table, shoving, until another intervened, drawing one of them away, murmuring soothing sounds like a mother with a baby. It was bizarre, this conflict with few sound effects. Repressed violence.

"Is that good?" I asked Father Flaherty.

"Of course not. But meditation and prayer — there, I've been avoiding that word, but I mean prayer not to influence God to answer, but to produce a harmonious state of mind — such meditation and prayer provide an integration of the self and allow for the interaction of unrelated thoughts and feelings, even violence."

"You've got an answer for everything."

"Indeed, I've got damn few answers," he said tartly. "I've got lots of questions and a few observations, that's all."

I wasn't expecting any miracles, and there were none. I was drawn to what this man said, his theories and thoughts. And I was drawn as well to this place of solitude, this most Catholic of places, the monastery, a place which exemplified the forces I was trying to elude. I was like a salmon wriggling my way down the Corrib to Galway Bay, past the string of fishermen lining the banks, and I mistook my wriggling journey for real escape. I hadn't made it yet, and I wasn't likely to since my struggling seemed only to set the hook more firmly in my mouth.

Nothing much happened in the monastery, but time passed quickly, and I came to realize that this is so because the monastery does not provide an escape from life but a deep and searing confrontation with it, and it was this confrontation that made the time speed by.

When I faced this, I began to realize the value of reconciliation. I wanted to talk about my life, yet I wanted to be silent on specific acts.

"Is it possible to do that, Father?"

"Any attempt at reconciliation is good, even a first hesitating step."

"The thin edge of the wedge?"

"Something like that, to be sure. Maybe it'll never go farther."

"You're sneaky, Father."

"I try my best to be."

"You're kidding, right?"

He just smiled.

"A week ago," I said, "I would have laughed at the possibility of seeing myself in this position."

"You see it as a position of weakness, d'ye now?"

"I think...it's maybe...progress...."

Silence hung between us.

"I've done terrible things," I said. "To men, to women, to my fellow human beings."

I stopped, and he let the silence drag.

"Let me ask you a question, Father. If a child is being abused, is he justified in taking any means to stop it?"

"That depends."

"Are you sure you're not a Jesuit, Father?"

"I mean it's the old question of ends and means, isn't it? The end the child proposes is good, to stop the abuse. But it depends if the means he uses really serves the end and doesn't defeat it in any way."

"Can you explain that?"

"Certainly. You cannot use bad means to attain a good end. For example, men and governments in power often try to condone their use of violence towards individuals by making it appear that their injustice is for the common good — the good of all — and is therefore justified. But since social justice involves justice for all, a government which employs unjust means defeats the end it pretends to serve. You cannot use bad means to attain a good end any more than you can build a good house with bad materials."

We were just talking. There was nothing didactic in his

manner, yet nonetheless I felt my stomach sink.

"So the child might be wrong to kill his abuser?"

He looked at me strangely. "You could say that. He might also be right."

"And if a person killed another to save a friend from being killed, even though they were engaged in robbery, I suppose that too might be wrong?"

"Most likely — the old ends and means again."

"I see."

Again the silence dragged. After a bit he said, "D'ye suppose there might be any sorrow felt for these deeds?"

"For some, yes...but not all...not yet, anyway...."

He paused again then nodded.

"Some things take longer," he said.

"I may never...."

"I know." He tacked. "I've seen you at Mass."

"The externals — I have no feeling for them, but in my heart I have a rapport with the core of the Mass — the suffering and hope it contains. Am I being naive?"

"I don't know. But I hope you believe in prayer because that's what you're doing — whether you know it or not."

I smiled. "The salmon has been netted."

"What?"

"Nothing. Yes, I believe in prayer."

"You learned something then?"

"Not the least of which is that eventually one is forced to meet oneself in silence and in darkness...and that can be an unpleasant experience...yet strangely purifying."

He nodded. "D'ye think that long-lost youth can muster up an Act of Contrition?"

I began. "Oh my God, I am heartily sorry...." I stumbled in places, but I finished it. He touched my shoulder, repeated the time-worn phrase, "Go in peace and may God bless you."

I rose to go, and he walked with me to the door. I passed him an envelope.

"You don't have to—"

"Father, I've eaten your food, picked your brain, learned from both you and the solitude, and found forgiveness. I shall never have another experience as valuable as this. I should give you everything I own — but I'm not yet at that stage of perfection."

He smiled. "Don't get there. People will think you're crazy."

"Should I care what people think?"

He chuckled. That was it. We shook hands warmly. I packed my few bits of clothing and my shaving gear in my bag and left. The next day I departed Ireland for good.

CHAPTER 27

Is such a sudden conversion possible? Is it sudden, or is it even a conversion, or is it something I've been working towards for years? Has not God been hounding me, as Francis Thompson says, "...down the nights and down the days...and down the labyrinthine ways of my own mind..."?

There is a lightness of my being as if some great weight that has been pressing down on my chest all my life has been lifted. It's true — there is relief in confession.

Does it seem too easy? Not when one has lived with guilt and remorse for so long. No, it is not easy, nor is it easy to tamp down those old feelings which return to haunt me at moments of mental and spiritual weakness. No, it'll probably never be easy, but now in my more clear-headed moments, I know it will never be as bad as it once was.

It seems that the faces of the men I killed do not spring so readily into my conscious mind, but I notice that the shadowy images of the past are taking on the clarity of sharp photographs. Is this the way life happens, I wondered, with events of younger days coming into clearer focus? I always thought it was the other way round, that events became hazy, unreal, as if they were something that someone once talked about, that had happened to someone else. But no, the smooth-featured Peter Hogan turns up regularly in my dreams, and a wrinkled Aloysious Doyle — "old Doyle" still to me — even though I am now past the age he was when he died. Note "when he died," not "when I killed him." On such half-truths is life constructed.

I may well have to account for my sins in the heel of the hunt, but it seems to me that I have been doing so all along, that I am doing so now.

Now is the time to muster whatever faith I have. What was it Father Flaherty had said? Faith is not required to serve Mass, to attend bingo, to collect for church renovations. Faith is grand for the time of dying, but if we save up to use it only then, we shall be bankrupt in no time. Faith takes practice and must be developed in times of heartbreak, in times of bitterness, in times of anger, in times of doubt, in times of sorrow. He worked hard to convince me that faith is the only thing that will get us through to the end without madness. I believed him, yet, despite this conviction, I still lack the true faith of the believer, still employ cynicism and skepticism, always in the back of my mind thinking my faith would be there in the end when I needed it. I considered not the uselessness of a deathbed repentance. So I prayed for the faith I knew I was lacking, but probably ended up mustering nothing more than a bit of pious hope.

I had gotten away with murder not once, but twice. But really, I was coming to understand, I had gotten away with nothing. There was still a hole in my centre, in my heart, where feeling should be. Was it only my imagination, or was the hole getting smaller, closing over?

Such thoughts always brought me back to Emily Kate.

The last time she and I had talked, I had almost slipped up in the cardinal rule of the betrayer: you must start acting the moment you're challenged. Or, rather, you must never stop acting, not for an instant, ever, not even when you're alone in a room with the lights off and the covers over your head. This time I was ready. This time, I vowed, it would be different.

I wheeled my bag through Customs and into the arrival area. I saw her standing back, and when she caught my eye she waved. She was wearing a brown skirt and a checked turtleneck sweater under her open topcoat. She looked outdoorsy and lovely.

"Welcome back," she said. "You look like you had a good time."

"I did. It's a wonderful country."

"Did it feel like, well, home to you?"

We were both aware — we were always aware — of our orphan status, and of how that obscured our ethnic origins.

"It did, indeed," I said. "And I'm sure it would for you, too."

"Some day I may find out."

We were near the exit. There was a silence. How eerie they are, these silences that fall between intimates, making them strangers to each other. At such moments, anything might happen. A tender word and I might have admitted to that whole other life I was keeping from her, but I could not bring myself to go that far.

"When is your plane to the Island?" she asked.

"A couple of hours."

"We could go into Halifax — to my place."

"It's hardly worth it, you take the time in and out."

"Well...you could stay overnight. That is, if you don't have to be back today."

I stared at her. It *is* possible, I decided, to live apart, not to see one another for years, to climb two separate sets of steps towards life's end, then to come back together with a whole new set of understandings about each other. One must live a life to understand that, not merely play at youthful games that have no basis in reality.

"Would it be all right?"

"I wouldn't ask you if it wasn't."

"I suppose not. Look, Emily Kate, this takes some getting used to. Are you sure?"

"I'm sure. You can sleep in the spare room."

Just to remove any ambiguity about the arrangements, I thought, keeping my face blank.

"Sounds great to me," I said. "We can get caught up."

When we arrived, I threw my bag in on the bed and sat in the kitchen while she made tea. I stretched, relaxing.

"You seem more...peaceful," she said.

"I made a Retreat in Ireland."

"You! A Retreat! Impossible."

"I know, but — there you are."

"You're back in the Church?"

Quick, quick, sharp as a thornbush. I forced a laugh. "Oh, I wouldn't go that far."

"What then?"

"Don't mistake a plea for help with surrender."

"Did I hear you right? You asked for help? You? For what?"

I shrugged. "My life...my past...everything...."

She studied me for a few seconds. "You *have* changed."

"I know. I can feel it."

"This is not just another act?"

Acting with all my talents, I said, "No, I don't think so."

"You don't seem too sure."

"I'm not sure about much anymore, Emily Kate. Every year, it seems there are more things I'm not sure about. I'm becoming convinced that a wide-ranging uncertainty is the mark of the truly mature man."

She smiled. "You're probably right."

I was ready to ask her. I felt at ease, detached. I don't know what happens to me in times of crisis, but I have a way of going still all over, time seeming to move in slow motion. It's a change I've heard star athletes talk about. In moments of extreme stress, the play seems to slow down for them, they intuit what is developing, they know what moves to make. It is that quality that makes them stars. I hoped for no less.

Now I was acting for my life, for our life together, if we were ever to have one. I had the sense of levitating, of rising out of myself, of standing back and observing my performance.

"Do you think there's any way you might consider marriage to me, Emily Kate?"

There. It was said, done. Now what?

"This is rather sudden, isn't it?"

"Not for me. I've thought of it every day since that time I told you that no one would ever—"

"—ever love me as you do. I remember."

I took her in my arms, and we kissed long and ardently. She pushed back, stroking my face, green eyes flashing.

"You've achieved some tenderness in your new maturity," she said.

Is this what love is really for, I wondered, to lend us a new conception of ourselves? My voice sounded softer to me, my every action seemed informed by a melancholy grandeur. My smile, touched with sadness, was a calm benediction upon the world.

"I have, haven't I?" I said.

We sat there, saying nothing, saying everything. Even though nothing had happened, something had happened all the same. Love, I decided, like the punchline of a joke, is all in the timing.

I knew I had to tread carefully. How difficult it is never to make a slip, but I believed that mine, if any, had been minor. The lies, the lies within the lies, assisted by large moments of truth. I had played everything as perfectly as I could. Now it was up to her.

"I'm sorry for ever hurting you, Emily Kate. I'll make it up to you," I murmured aloud, and even I could detect, finally, my sincerity.

"I believe you," she said. "And, yes, I'll marry you."

I took her in my arms again. This time there was no hesitation.

CHAPTER 28

My attempts at writing fiction have taken an almost com-
ical turn, probably due to my sense of inner freedom,
dare I say light-heartedness. Sometimes I entertain myself
by plotting impossible stories like the following:

> *Maeve, a well-to-do widow who has inherited the miserly*
> *savings of her animal-stuffing husband, doesn't know that*
> *Vespasian, the underworld veterinarian (who specializes in*
> *altering the looks of poodles to give them that thoroughbred*
> *air), is the son of Gemini Gina, the psychiatrist treating*
> *Maeve's son, Danny Boy Durkin, a well-known singer.*
> *Clarissa, the talent scout with the deaf dog, is married to*
> *Clarence, who is being chased by Sally, the waitress, whose*
> *friend, Madge, is an ambulance driver but also Vespasian's*
> *true love. Meanwhile, Xena, who is Vespasian's sister and*
> *Gemini Gina's daughter, attends a singles party, meets*
> *Harold, and becomes interested in becoming a cosmetician*
> *of the dead....*

I find this sort of thing interesting, time-consuming,
and useless, but it has a kind of gamesmanship to it, a paint-
by-numbers flavour, as I attempt to keep all the players in
their proper slots with thumbnail descriptions as a test of my
ability to isolate them. For example, "...skinny, wild-haired
Gina"; "...stolid, plodding Vespasian, his thick English accent
as substantial as his girth and better understood by his dogs
than by people"; "...they called her Sally the Flit..."; "...Danny
Boy knew enough never to reach for a high note, and when
requests came, as they always did, for his namesake song, he
would recite the words in the manner of George Burns or the

Pope, but not nearly as good as either of them...."

What I particularly liked about all this was that when I was fully involved in writing, my guilt, the everlasting weight in the pit of my stomach, disappeared. I hated returning to the real world, for, like most Irish Catholics, I am a Manichean by temperament: acceptance of the imperfectability of man is part of my DNA.

I always keep in mind that fakery is the very heart and soul of fiction. All our stories are nothing but a pack of lies, and the purpose of the research we do is not to make our stories real, but to make them appear real.

When I transfer this principle to my personal actions, I suppose I could be said to be a case of life imitating art.

To remain alive and active, I am convinced, we must always be reinventing ourselves, weaving new themes into our self-narrative, aware of our past, yet replanning our future, constantly revising the myth by which we live. We should expect no less of ourselves, and if it's a lie we are living, by our constancy to it, we make it the truth.

Emily Kate and I were married in St. Dunstan's Basilica and had our reception at the Charlottetown Hotel, which seemed such a large part of my destiny. It seemed fitting, somehow, and I attempted to explain this to our few guests as I offered a toast "to the Charlottetown Hotel." I caught the sly glances of a couple of them who were thinking, "Aha, he's on the sauce again." But I wasn't, and I haven't been for some time. I got tired of fighting booze, just as I got tired of fighting God. I said, "I quit. You win." And I found in both cases as time went by that by surrendering, I had won. This, I discovered, is the only battle you win by losing. You admit defeat, that you can no longer run your life by yourself, that you need help, and there it is. A bonus was that the doctor reported that as long as I practised "extreme moderation," there was little danger of my liver damage becoming more extensive.

Does it sound easy? Believe me, it's not — and it wasn't and isn't — but you do it a day at a time, an hour at a time, a minute at a time, if necessary. Faith is something you can call on at any time.

I discovered something else. You may be only acting that you have this faith, but it makes no difference — it's there anyway. It's part of your being. The lie becomes the reality.

CHAPTER 29

Emily Kate and I were married for ten years, the happiest years of my life. She'd moved from Halifax and we'd bought a small house in Charlottetown. In that time I never told her about the murders. There was always that unfinished business between us. I was sure God had forgiven me my sins, and I'd forgiven myself long ago, but I had never asked Emily Kate's forgiveness. During most of those ten years I didn't feel I needed to. The need, the desire grew steadily. But how could I tell her? How could I come to her after all these years and tell her the truth about what I'd denied so vehemently years before? All our years together, all our happiness, had been based on my convincing her of my innocence. How could I now go to her and tell her I'd lied to her, that I'd been acting? I couldn't do it, yet I knew I must.

I wrestled with this for months. Once, Emily Kate suggested I move out if I couldn't be more civil. I knew I was a trial and apologized, a thing I was doing a lot of lately. Finally, one day, Emily Kate sat me down and said, "I think you'd better talk about it."

It was as simple and as difficult as that.

The whole sad, sordid story spilled out of me. Of my suspicions about old Doyle being my father, of the beatings, the abuse, the poisoning. She hadn't even suspected this, only that perhaps I'd robbed him. About the old grocer, Hogan, and how I'd been there, wielding the knife until Frankie took it from me, of how I was sure one of my slashes had been the cause of his death. Of how I'd used Billy, forcing him into suicide.

She sat opposite me, watching me, nodding occasionally, saying nothing. Only her eyes expressed anything, and they slowly grew as cold as a January morning. I ran on and on, unable to look into those eyes, ending piteously, "You were right about me, Emily Kate, but I've changed. Please forgive me. I love you, you know I love you. It would be easy for me to say I denied all this to spare you the hurt — and that's true — but mostly I did it to spare myself — from your scorn, your anger, your leaving me. But I can't live with it any longer. Please, please forgive me."

They say people who receive a sudden shock look and act quite normal until the reality sinks in. It was that way with Emily Kate. She sat there for ten seconds, saying nothing, then her face began to break apart. Her voice was scarcely audible. "It was all a lie," she whispered.

The desire for self-preservation is strong and I now regretted my outburst. I was losing her, I could see it in her face. She shook her head. "How could you—? Why did you wait to tell me now?"

She rose and stumbled upstairs. It was no good going after her. She'd have to work this out by herself.

An hour later she came down with a bag. "I'm leaving," she said. Her eyes were red.

"Don't, Emily Kate. Please don't. I beg you."

She shook her head. "It's all been a lie. All of it."

"No," I said. "Not all. I love you, I've always loved you. That's no lie. The other, yes, but I was afraid of losing you."

"And you've succeeded. My God, I had no idea—. I've been living with a monster."

"How can you say that? Hasn't our life been good?"

"A lie!"

"No. That was the real me."

"'The real you'! Does anybody know the real you? Do even *you* know the real you? You had me fooled completely. How can you expect me to forgive you now?"

"I thought — after all these years — we've been happy...."

"I should have listened to my instincts back then. I knew, I just knew, you weren't as innocent as you said. But — you convinced me. I don't know, maybe I wanted to be convinced."

I hung my head. What was there to say? What was done was done.

She picked up her bag and started for the door. "Where will you go?" I said.

"Somewhere. I'll be back for my things sometime you're not here."

And she was gone. I stood rooted where I'd been since we started, leaning over, one hand now supporting my weight on the kitchen table, the other holding my stomach in case I heaved. I felt as if someone had just worked me over with a club. My foolish, foolish mouth. How could I have been so wrong? My happiness over the years had lulled me into a false sense of security. And the slight relief I felt at confessing was now overpowered by my enormous sense of loss. My confessions were finished — I'd nothing left to confess — but now I'd lost the dearest thing in the world to me — Emily Kate's love.

✻

Time passed. One month, six months, a year. One good thing, I held on. I did not slide back into my old habits. I was too old, too fixed now in my older, more mature, ways.

I didn't call her, she didn't call me. There was no contact.

Then, one day, two years later, I ran into her quite accidentally and quite literally in the local Co-op. I was hustling down an aisle and made a turn at the end and our carts collided.

"Oh, sorry," I said before I realized who it was. "Oh, Emily Kate. I *am* sorry."

She looked at me but said nothing. I saw the tightness of

her lips.

"It was an accident," I said. "I didn't even know you were in the store."

"I'm sure."

"It's true. But you believe what you want."

"I usually do," she said with a slight lifting at the corners of her mouth.

"I promise not to run into you in the parking lot," I said.

"Are your promises worth much these days?"

"As much as they always were — where you're concerned."

Her eyes gave me nothing.

"Nice talking to you," I said, nodding. I made to go.

"Nice talking to *you*," she said, her voice thawing a little.

It wasn't much, two ships in the night, but it was one of the most important exchanges in my life, because it gave me hope. Hope, the one thing we cannot live without. Each day, hope is reborn — this is the day that will be better, the day that the ache in the pit of my stomach disappears, the day that Emily Kate once more laughs with me, the day, maybe, that I won't think of her, the day that provides the fresh start.

No, it wasn't much, but I'd get by on that. It would keep me going, if necessary, for another two years.

I'd win her back, I knew it.

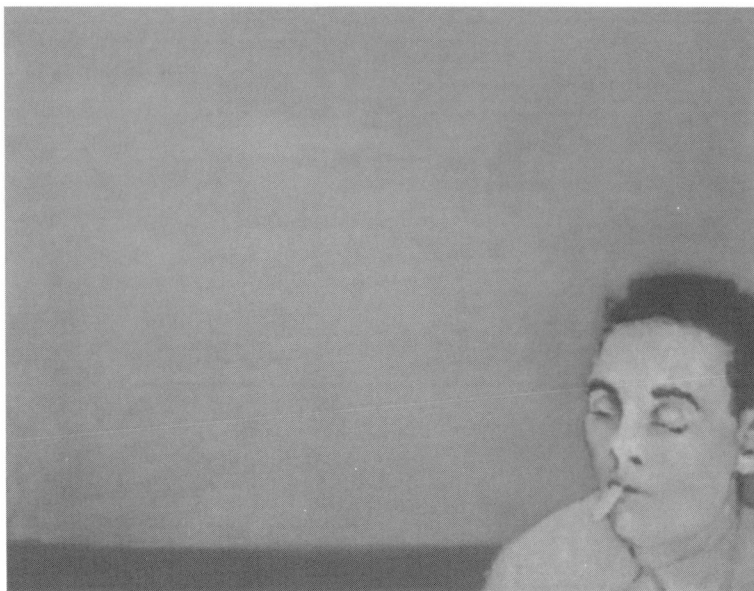

About the cover

Colourful Character, oil on canvas, by Brian Burke. Brian Burke lives with his wife Judith Scherer-Burke at Dalvay-by-the-Sea, Prince Edward Island. His paintings can be found in art galleries and private collections across North America and Europe.

The painting has been modified for graphic considerations.